The Embroidered Corpse

Brian Kavanagh

BeWrite Books
www.bewrite.net

Published internationally by BeWrite Books, UK.
32 Bryn Road South, Wigan, Lancashire, WN4 8QR.

A CIP catalogue record for this book is available from the British Library

ISBN-10: 1-905202-36-9
ISBN-13: 978-1-905202-36-2

First published in Australia by Jacobyte Books, 2002

Also available in eBook format from www.bewrite.net

Digitally produced by BeWrite Books

Cover art © Liz Miller 2006
emiller_domrep@hotmail.com

About the author

Brian Kavanagh has many years' experience in the Australian Film Industry in areas of production, direction, editing and writing. His editing credits include *The Chant Of Jimmie Blacksmith, Odd Angry Shot, The Devil's Playground, Long Weekend, Sex Is A Four-Letter Word* and the recent comedy, *Dags*. He received a Lifetime Achievement Award from the Australian Film Editors Guild and an Australian Film Institute award for Best Editing for *Frog Dreaming*. His first feature film which he produced and directed, *A City's Child*, won an AFI award for actress Monica Maughan and was screened at the London Film Festival as well as Edinburgh, Montreal, Chicago and Adelaide, where it won the Gold Southern Cross Advertiser Award for Best Australian Film.

Also by Brian Kavanagh:
Capable of Murder, 2005, BeWrite Books

The Embroidered Corpse

One

'Some days, I could just murder you!'

'Mark, you say that at least once a week.' Belinda smiled at his reflection in the mirror. He sat leaning against the bed head, arms stretched behind his head. His bare chest rising above the crumpled sheets was still brown from the past summer.

'Well, you drive me mad.'

Belinda dropped her robe and, teasingly, reached for her bra. 'With desire?'

Mark considered her sleek figure. 'Well, with that too, but what I mean is, this crazy trip to York.'

Belinda finished dressing. 'It's not crazy. We're going to the antique fair at Castle Howard.'

'But you've got responsibilities here.' Mark gestured towards the window. 'The house. The garden. The tourists.'

Belinda looked out the window onto the garden below. The last of the autumn leaves had fallen. The bare Elm trees, their skeletal limbs stark against the sky, reminded her of the garden the first time she'd seen it. It had been a ruin then. The death of her aunt had brought the inherited pleasures of ownership of the cottage and garden, plus a healthy bank-balance.

'I've arranged for Mrs Edwards to take care of the coaches. Besides, in a week or so, the tours finish for the season.'

'I would have thought, after going to the trouble and expense of restoring the damned thing, you'd want to be here.'

'Mark, the tourists come to see the garden that Capability Brown created, not to see me.'

'But –'

'But nothing. You're just being petulant because I'm going away for a couple of nights.'

Mark tugged at the sheets. Belinda was right of course, but he'd never admit it.

'I'm not sure I like you gadding about–'

'Gadding about? You're getting quainter by the minute.'

'– with that woman.'

'If you mean Hazel, *say* Hazel. Not "that woman".'

'She's a bad influence.'

'You sound like a maiden aunt.'

'She's a tart, and you know it.'

'Now you sound like a prudish maiden aunt. OK, so Hazel likes the blokes. What's so wrong with that? I like you.'

'God knows what sort of things she'll get up to in York,' Mark grumbled.

'I don't think there's much to get up to in York. And what about you? You're always gadding about, as you call it.'

'Selling houses means I have to travel.'

'Well, we buy and sell antiques, remember?'

Her friendship with the older, more capricious, and gregarious Hazel Whitby had given her a different slant on life – and how it was to be lived. It was this influence that Mark objected to.

A deafening squeal of brakes interrupted the discussion as a large tourist coach came to a halt outside the cottage. Belinda glanced out the window. The coach door opened and a mere handful of middle-aged men and women emerged, followed by a small group of giggling Japanese girls.

Belinda gave a grunt. 'Sometimes I wonder if tourists will ever travel again. Mad cows. Terrorists. Maybe I should pack it in and head home to Melbourne. At least there …' She smiled at some secret antipodean memory.

Mark frowned. He didn't like the idea of her returning to Australia. For a number of reasons.

The tour guide, a young woman in a vivid yellow uniform,

gathered her brood together and began her lecture. She pointed at the house. Tourist eyes followed her finger and the first of many cameras emerged from under cover.

Belinda drew back from the window and picked up her overnight bag. 'You'd better get dressed. They'll be inside soon. We don't want a repeat of last week.'

Mark smiled as he recalled the look on the woman's face. The tourist had strayed from the designated area downstairs into the private quarters upstairs. Her scream as Mark stepped from the shower had brought the tour guide running and added a certain piquancy to an otherwise dull day.

'What do you expect to get out of the fair?' Mark threw back the covers, not bothering to cover his nakedness.

Belinda smiled at his display. 'Don't think that'll work, mate.'

Mark raised an amused eyebrow. 'It has before.'

'Maybe, darling, but not now – I'm off.' Belinda blew him a kiss and left the room. Laughing to herself, she ran lightly down the stairs. It was the phone call last night that was bothering him. Returning from a dinner to celebrate Mark's thirtieth birthday, Belinda had received a call from Brad, her old boyfriend in Australia. They'd chatted on for over an hour while Mark, ostentatiously flipping through worn copies of *Country Life*, failed to hide the fact that he was listening to every word. Mark was jealous! How pleasing.

Mark punched the mattress with his fist, then clambered across the bed to the window to watch her departure. Below, Hazel's Mercedes was pulling up. Hazel, now divorced from the formidable Mr Whitby, had profited monstrously by playing upon her ex-husband's guilt; he had decamped with a nubile beauty from a travel agency while booking a second honeymoon for himself and Hazel. The astutely new-found wealth not only enabled her to expand her interest in *objets d'art*, but freed her to enhance her already considerable intimacy with – as she lasciviously called them – "hunks". By this, she meant any man under the age of forty and preferably those given to athletics, not necessarily of the Olympic persuasion. A moment later Belinda emerged from the house and threaded her way through the tourists. She exchanged a greeting with the tour guide and without looking back got into the waiting car. Then she was gone.

Mark became aware of excited chatter. He also became aware that he was standing at the window. Naked. The click of camera shutters attended him as he hurriedly pulled the blind.

After attending the Castle Howard Antiques Fair, Belinda and Hazel made their way home though the early November gloom towards Somerset. Hazel's years of experience in buying and selling Georgian silver had whetted her appetite for expansion and she had branched out into sixteenth to eighteenth century household furniture. Her enthusiasm had infected Belinda, and the younger woman was a ready pupil. Today's fair had proved enlightening, and the lure and romance of antiques overwhelmed her.

When darkness fell, a stopover at a small country pub seemed the right thing to do. After inspecting their rooms, Hazel, as though guided by some in-built radar, led the way to the bar. And to Joe the barman.

As she sipped her drink and watched Hazel weave her charm on Joe, Belinda smiled to herself and reflected on the events that had brought Hazel and Mark into her life.

After her formative years in Australia, Belinda had settled into her new life in England in the village of Milford. Her cottage on the outskirts of Bath, although dating in part from the thirteenth century, was of little merit. It was the garden recently restored to the original design by famed English landscape designer Capability Brown that was the main attraction. A small garden designed by this genius was a rarity, so its rediscovery had set the horticultural world agog. Hazel had replenished the house with the appropriate fittings and furnishings of the period, and the two women had entered into an agreement to share the not insignificant profits from the endless coach-loads of snooping tourists that descended daily through the summer months.

At the same time Belinda had met Mark Sallinger, who seemed keen to buy the house. But instead he'd fallen in love with her.

The two women differed not only in disposition and interests but also physically. Belinda, with her long slender legs, slim build, short dark hair and blue eyes, had the relaxed stride of a feline that came from her years in Australia and the casual way of life there. Somehow the cramped environment of Europe had not restricted her frame of mind and she carried her twenty-six years with an ease and vitality that added to her physical beauty.

Hazel, on the other hand, openly described herself as "mutton dressed as lamb" and although Belinda thought this to be too critical a description, there was no doubting that the older woman had seen her best days. However, this did not deter her. If gravity and time were her natural enemies, she laughed in their faces and proceeded to disguise their inroads on her form with liberal use of dyes and pigments that deluded the observer into thinking her no more than forty-five. In a dim light.

Belinda was brought back to the present by a lecherous laugh from Hazel.

'If it's antiques you want, you ought to pay a visit to Kidbrooke House.' Joe placed a fresh gin and tonic on the bar.

'And what makes you think I'd be interested in Kidbrooke House?' smiled Hazel, whose interest at the moment lay strictly within the confines of the cosy hotel and hopefully within the even more snug embrace of Joe's muscular arms.

'Got some nice pieces there, I can tell you.' His eyes strayed over Hazel Whitby's obvious charms.

Hazel turned to Belinda. 'Might as well check it out. Nothing ventured, nothing gained.'

Belinda was not so sure she was referring to Kidbrooke House.

The Mercedes came to a halt outside a large thatched Tudor house. The sign before it read: *"Kidbrooke House; open to the public every day except Christmas Day"*.

The two-storeyed half-timber and brick structure stood well back from the road. Wisteria, now bare and inert, twined around the façade. A dovecote stood nearby. Belinda warmed to the seventeenth century house, imagining the history it had seen; the people who had lived and died there; the romance of centuries past. Smoke from a large chimney drifted lazily into the winter morning sky and tiny birds sought refuge in the overhanging eaves. The glowing red bricks and tiles of the structure looked out over well-kept part-terraced gardens in which an elderly white-haired man was pottering. The man had a dignified, almost regal, bearing and although his clothes were a trifle shabby, he wore them as though they had just been delivered fresh and new from his tailor. As the two women approached, he looked up eagerly.

'He must be the guide,' said Hazel, wondering if he would expect a tip. To the man she said: 'We want to look over the house. Is that all right?'

The man dropped a spade and wiped his hands on a large red towel. 'By all means, madam. I'd be delighted to show you and your daughter through.'

Belinda bit her lip and swallowed her laughter. Hazel wracked her brain for a biting reply but, stunned by the man's assumption, she meekly followed him towards the house. The front door opened into one large, open hall. A compact dogleg staircase led to the first floor. Chattering on in an endless established patter, the man led them from room to room.

'It was built in 1602 by the ninth Earl but was enlarged by the third Duke. A costly exercise because when he'd finished, the expenses were so great, the Duke left liabilities of £160,000.' The old man chuckled. 'That accounts for the house being thrown open to the public. Family debts are always with us.'

Lagging behind, Hazel enviously eyed several pieces of

Jacobean and Elizabethan furniture. 'I'd kill to get my hands on some of this stuff,' she whispered to Belinda as she caught up. 'And that Sèvres porcelain would fetch a fortune. But I think *two* Canalettos is stretching credulity,' she concluded archly.

A framed tapestry portraying a mediaeval king seated on his throne took Belinda's attention. 'This must be very old?'

'Well, it's a bit of a mystery to me. Where it came from, I mean.' The old man wiped his glasses on a spotless handkerchief and peered at the square of framed tapestry that hung above the Jacobean cabinet. 'It certainly reminds one of the Bayeux Tapestry, at least in style.' He waved a finger at the embroidered king. 'That's supposed to be William the Conqueror; and it does have a definite mediaeval flavour.' He reached over with a gnarled hand and lifted the frame from the wall. 'But I see that the glass is cracked. I must have it repaired.' He sighed at the thought of the anticipated expense.

'May I have a closer look, please?' Intrigued, Belinda put out her hand to receive the framed tapestry. About a foot or so square, the faded tapestry showed a crowned figure seated beneath a structure representing a church. A Latin inscription read HICRE SIDET: WILLELM REX: AN GLORIUM. Beneath was the embroidered figure of what appeared to be the corpse of a monk in the process of being buried, and some half-unstitched skulls and bones.

Hazel snorted her contempt. 'Probably only a Victorian copy. Like the one at Reading. Those frustrated females spent their lives forever stitching ugly bits of tat.'

'Oh, I'm certain it's not Victorian,' said the man, throwing her a disparaging glance. 'Probably done about late eighteenth century or very early in the nineteenth. It's been in our family since 1832, or so the records tell me.'

Belinda and Hazel looked at the man with new respect. Hazel cleared her throat. 'Sorry,' she muttered apologetically, 'we thought you were the attendant.'

The old man chuckled. 'Most people make that mistake. But no, this is my family home. And I enjoy showing people around. It fills in the day. At my age you look for distractions to make the minutes left to you more appealing.'

'I don't suppose that you'd care to sell this?' Belinda asked tentatively. The tapestry had struck a chord in her and she longed to own it. Yet even as she said the words a sudden spasm of intense grief overcame her as though she had been touched by the iniquities of past centuries.

The man smiled regretfully and shook his head. 'I'm afraid not.' He took the frame with the broken glass from Belinda's reluctant hand. 'Everything will remain here at least until I die. After that ...' He shrugged. 'Well, after that I imagine it will all be sold.'

Hazel's ears pricked up. 'How so?'

The man opened a drawer in the Jacobean cabinet and slipped the framed tapestry inside. With a push that suggested finality he shut the drawer tight. 'I am, I'm sad to say, the last of my line. There are no more William de Montforts left. William was always the name given to the eldest son and heir. That is my name, but alas, I have no heir, no son. And I am the last of my family.'

Belinda felt a wave of compassion for the old man. 'That's so sad.'

He cast watery eyes onto her. 'Sad? Yes, but the way of the world.' His glance took in the ancient room. 'I can only hope that whoever acquires the property and possessions treasures them as I have done.'

William de Montfort accompanied the two women out into the garden and they said their farewells. He waved to them as Hazel started the engine. Belinda waved back.

As they drew away from the house, a small black car pulled up. Two figures emerged and approached the house. Belinda was surprised to see that they were monks, both wearing long grey habits tied at the waist with rope. Both had very close-cropped hair.

'That's something you don't often see these days.'

'What?' Hazel's eye was on passing traffic.

'Monks. And very young monks at that. They can't be more than twenty or so.'

Hazel grunted and turned the car onto the main road. Monks were not in her scheme of things. Competition with a possessive wife was one thing but she drew the line at fighting Holy Mother Church.

As they sped off Belinda glanced back over her shoulder at the house. She glimpsed the two monks talking to William. As they went out of her sight she saw that the three men were arguing violently. One of the monks was extremely aggressive.

The car hummed along the highway as Belinda and Hazel made their way south to Lincoln. Belinda found that her thoughts kept returning to the framed portion of tapestry. It had a strange fascination for her and she could not put it out of her mind.

'He said it looked like the Bayeux Tapestry, didn't he?' she said, as she popped a sticky caramel into her mouth.

'What?'

Belinda forced her jaws apart, the adhesive caramel cementing them together. 'William de thingummy,' she said with difficulty.

'Who?'

Belinda swallowed and pushed the gooey caramel into her cheek. 'William de whatever. The old man at Kidbrooke House.'

'Oh, him. Yes, he did.'

Hazel's attention was given to overtaking a large pantechnicon, no doubt returning antiques from the Fair, and for a few moments Belinda shrank down in her seat and silently offered up a prayer for their survival.

'It certainly looks like the Bayeux Tapestry, or at least in the same style,' Hazel shouted through the roar of competing engines.

Belinda opened her eyes to find the large van securely behind them. She relaxed a little and squirmed upright in her seat. 'From what I remember of English History, the tapestry is about the Norman invasion of 1066. Now it's kept in France. In Bayeux. Right?'

'Aren't *you* a fountain of knowledge. At the Grand Séminaire. It used to be at the cathedral and only dragged out on feast days.'

'How big is it?' Belinda sucked at a fragment of caramel that was bonded to her tooth.

'How the hell should I know? Fifty, sixty metres or something like that. But why this sudden interest in the Bayeux Tapestry?'

Belinda thought for a moment. 'I'm not sure. It's just that the bit we saw at Kidbrooke House interests me. And I thought I'd like to see it, the Tapestry I mean. But that means a trip to France.'

Hazel glanced in the rear vision mirror at a snappy sports car that was rapidly overtaking them. 'Well, you can always see the fake one at Reading.'

Belinda was suddenly alert. 'That's right. You mentioned it before. You said it was Victorian.'

'That's right,' replied Hazel, her eyes skimming over the young male driver of the sports car as it recklessly zoomed past. She gave a slight sigh.

Belinda, who hadn't noted her companion's distraction, had a sudden idea. She rummaged in the glove compartment for a road map. 'Hazel. Let's go see it.'

'What?'

'The fake Bayeux Tapestry. At Reading.'

Hazel glanced at her watch. 'It's a bit out of our way.'

'No it's not,' cried Belinda excitedly, tracing a route on the map. 'We just veer off a bit after Lincoln and head south to Reading. We can have lunch there, see the tapestry and be back home in Bath before nightfall.'

Hazel sighed in exasperation. After all this driving she wanted to soak in a hot tub with a cool drink in her hand. 'Well, all right,' she muttered grudgingly, 'but you can pay for lunch. And by that I don't mean pub grub.'

The replica of the eleventh century tapestry extended its full seventy metres. As she walked along the length of the embroidery, Belinda began to feel involved in the unfolding drama, the drama of one of the most legendary events in the history of England, the Norman Invasion of William the Conqueror. She saw the representation of Harold swearing allegiance to William – Harold enthroned as King of England – William learning of Harold's accession – the Normans arriving at Pevensey and attacking the English – climaxing with Harold being slaughtered on the battlefield at Hastings.

There the duplicate tapestry came to an abrupt end with the English army in flight.

'But what happened?' exclaimed Belinda. 'Why isn't it finished? Did those Victorian ladies run out of cotton?'

'It's as complete as it is, my dear. No one knows if the original was ever completed or if part of it, the end of the story if you like, is missing. And that's not the only thing missing,' Hazel concluded with a snigger. Always observant where men were concerned, she pointed to the stitched outline of a naked man. 'He's lacking his fundamentals.'

Belinda saw that the Victorian embroiderers had castrated the man with needle and thread. 'Oh, I see. Queen Victoria was not permitted to be amused.'

Hazel allowed Belinda to purchase a booklet that told the story and history of the Bayeux tapestry, then herded her back to the car and set off for home. Belinda saw little of the journey. The limited information in the book fascinated her. When she retired that night in her home at Milford she read the contents for the third time.

The next morning Belinda opened the newspaper as she sipped her first cup of tea for the day. The usual government debacles, plus the latest frivolous antics of a young woman once remotely connected with the Royal Family, completed the headlines. Belinda was just about to turn the page when a small item at the bottom claimed her attention. As she read it she felt a chill of apprehension.

MAN FOUND MURDERED

Police last night were baffled by the unexplained death of William de Montfort, whose body was found in his ancestral home of Kidbrooke House in Yorkshire.

Mr de Montfort, whose family has been in the area for four hundred years, was discovered in a pool of blood by visitors on a day-tour to the historical house.

Police are treating the case as one of murder but have not been able to establish a motive for the killing. A police spokesman said it was a particularly violent crime and they are looking for a sadistic murderer.

The tour guide who found the body revealed Mr de Montfort had been stabbed in the eye and his thigh slashed.

Two

The ancient city of Wells lay before her, with the Cathedral dominating the skyline. Six hundred saintly stone eyes watched as Belinda entered the market place. Ahead she saw Hazel engaged in conversation with a sign-writer, while workmen carefully unloaded a few pieces of antique furniture. Hazel had taken a lease on this shop in Wells to handle the Jacobean, Elizabethan and Georgian furniture exclusively, keeping her small shop in Bath for her silver and bric-a-brac.

Parking her car, Belinda hurried to her friend. The sign-writer turned his attention to Hazel's window and set about practising his gilded craft.

'He's been murdered!'

Hazel's attention was on the safe advent of a Chippendale chair. 'There'll be a murder here if that chair is scratched.'

Belinda waved the newspaper under Hazel's nose. 'Will you listen to me? Read this.'

Hazel took the paper and glanced at the article Belinda was pointing at.

'William de Thingummy. He's dead.'

Hazel read the article in silence and handed the paper back to Belinda. 'So?'

Belinda gave an exasperated sigh. 'But don't you see? He was murdered. And it must have happened just after we left Kidbrooke House.'

Hazel thought this through as she entered the shop. 'And this affects us how?'

Hazel's indifference began to annoy Belinda. 'Well, only in as much as we were probably the last people to see him alive.'

'Supposition. You have no proof of that. And even if we were, again I ask, how does it affect us?'

For a moment Belinda was stumped for a reply. How did it affect her? In truth she could find no answer, short of the shock of the old man's murder and a genuine sorrow at his death.

'Well, it doesn't really, I suppose. Except that I am sure it happened just after we left him, and as he said, he was the last of his line and to die such a horrible death ... well, it upsets me, that's all.'

A gleam on interest sprang into Hazel's eyes. 'That's right.' She gave a self-satisfied laugh.

'What do you mean?'

Hazel busied herself with rearranging a nest of tables. 'As you said, he was the last of his line.'

'And?'

'And that means, now he's dead his possessions will be sold.' She turned to Belinda with a look of triumph. 'And I intend to buy some.'

The steak and kidney pudding served at the Red Lion hotel was cooked to perfection and both Belinda and Hazel sighed contentedly as they pushed their plates away. The crowded luncheon cabal was beginning to clear as the locals went back to their various jobs. A few late tourists lingered, like so many transmigratory birds that had missed the opportunity to fly to warmer climes.

'Why would anyone want to murder the old man?'

Hazel, who was rereading the newspaper's report of the crime, shook her head in response. She reached for her glass of port. 'Who knows? These days they'll kill you for the price of a Big Mac.'

Belinda took up the paper. 'It was a particularly violent attack. To stab him in the eye and then slash his thigh. Why go to such extremes?'

'Perhaps the old man put up a fight. Tried to defend himself and whoever attacked him had to fight him off and in the process messed him about a bit.'

'They certainly did that. If they were going to rob him they could have just tied him up or bopped him on the head. But to mutilate him? It seems inhuman.'

'I thought all murder was inhuman. Besides, you said we were the last to see him alive.'

'Well, we probably were.'

Hazel shook her head. 'Always assuming that the murder took place soon after we were at the house, we were not the last to see him.'

'How do you know?'

'You've forgotten the monks.' Hazel gave her a superior look and swallowed the last of her port.

'The monks. Yes. I'd forgotten them,' said Belinda. Then she shook her head. 'But monks wouldn't murder an old man.'

'I didn't say they did,' replied Hazel as she reapplied lipstick. 'I just suggested that they would have seen him after us. But you're wrong, you know.'

'Why?'

'Just because they're monks doesn't exclude them from being murderers.'

The auction of William de Montfort's possessions was held in the large entrance hall of Kidbrooke House and although the crowd was small it was obvious early on to Hazel that they knew their business. She also realised that she was up against formidable opponents and that her limited funds would be a severe stumbling block.

'Isn't it rather unusual to hold the auction at the house?' asked Belinda, 'I thought these affairs were held in auction rooms.'

Hazel gave her makeup a last minute maintenance tune up and nodded her head. 'Old Mr de Thingummy ...'

'De Montfort,' murmured Belinda, feeling that the old man deserved a little respect, certainly at the scene of his death.

'Whatever,' mumbled Hazel, as she placed her compact in her handbag. 'It seems that he requested it in his will. That any sale of his family's property should take place in the house and not in some place soiled by commerce. The auctioneer's firm told me,' she ended in answer to Belinda's questioning look.

She and Belinda took their place at the back of the group and sat through the initial bidding as, one by one, the treasures of Kidbrooke House were sold off. But search as she might through the catalogue, Belinda could find no reference to the mediaeval tapestry.

The prices for the paintings took Belinda's breath away and even Hazel found the palms of her hands sweaty with nerves. More than anything she wished she had access to a double gin and tonic. She had earmarked three items, a seventeenth century closet stool, a Georgian table and a Jacobean cabinet.

The auctioneer, with syrupy voice, confirmed that King Charles I had used the closet stool during his time in York at the time of the Civil War. The embroidered crimson velvet box was put on display midst the oohs and ahhs of the assembly. Hazel looked grim-faced when, early on, she was forced out of the bidding and lost it to an effete collector who, having got what he came for, left with his ornate companion.

Hazel could barely contain her ill will. 'Well, at least it's staying in a royal family.'

Belinda felt confused. She hadn't discovered what the function of the object was. 'What on earth was it? What would King Charles have done with it?'

Hazel fanned herself flamboyantly with the catalogue. 'It was the throne, dear. The Royal Loo.'

Belinda smiled and looked over her shoulder at the departing couple. Near the door stood a young man dressed soberly in a dark suit. His attention was distracted and he glanced across at Belinda. He held her gaze for a moment and then switched his focus back to the auctioneer.

Belinda too turned back but she wore a frown. She felt certain that she had seen the young man somewhere before. She stole another glance at him but he had gone.

Hazel nudged her excitedly as bidding began on the Jacobean cabinet. Several times in the next few minutes Hazel's spirits soared and sank in rapid succession but with a clap of her hands she echoed the bang of the auctioneer's gavel marking the sale down to her.

Belinda congratulated her distractedly, because the realisation had dawned that the young man in the dark suit, the young man that had stood behind her, the young man with the short cut hair, was the aggressive monk who had visited Kidbrooke House on the day of the murder.

On the return journey to Bath, Hazel, fixed buoyantly behind the steering wheel, was exuberantly extolling the beauty of the Jacobean cabinet and although the failure to secure the closet stool still rankled, she had gained the Georgian table so that her cup, if not overflowing, was at least filled to the brim.

Belinda, on the other hand was subdued and thoughtful, only answering Hazel's excited chatter with an occasional 'yes' or 'no'. Hazel grew resentful at this lack of enthusiasm. She glanced across at Belinda. 'What on earth's the matter with you, Missy? You've been in a purple fog since we left the auction.'

Belinda looked at her and gave a weak smile. 'I'm sorry, Hazel. I'm really very happy for you and I'm delighted that you got what you wanted. Except for the Royal Loo.'

Hazel grimaced and pushed her foot hard onto the accelerator. 'Yes, well. The less said about that the better.'

'It's just that …' Belinda hesitated.

Hazel snorted. 'Oh, for God's sake, spit it out. What's bothering you?'

Belinda drew in her breath. 'There was a man there. At the auction.'

'Sweetheart, there were a lot of men there, believe me, I saw them. Excluding the couple who got the loo, that is. More like ladies of quality.'

'Hazel, be serious. I'm talking about one particular man. He was one of the monks.'

Hazel sighed. 'Oh, we're not on about that again are we?'

Belinda twisted in her seat to face her. 'Believe me, I'm certain that the man at the auction was at the house the day of the murder.'

'I didn't see anyone in a monk's habit.'

Belinda shook her head. 'No. He was in a suit. A dark suit and he had short hair …'

'Wait a minute,' interrupted Hazel. 'Are you telling me that just because you saw a man with short hair, he automatically qualifies to be a monk? And not just any monk, but one you saw weeks ago, *glimpsed* weeks ago from a moving car?'

Belinda sank back in her seat. 'I know it sounds odd …'

'Odd? Try bizarre.'

'Well, in a way it is bizarre. Hazel, I'm certain it was the same man. OK, I only had a glimpse of him the first time, but that was enough. And I'd know him again. What's more, it's conceivable he was the murderer. You yourself said that it was not impossible for a monk to commit murder.'

'Well,' replied Hazel acidly, 'there's only one thing left for you to do, isn't there? You must go to the police.'

Belinda gave her a black look but did not reply. Hazel glanced at her with a triumphant expression. 'No, you can't do that can you? Because what real evidence do you have? Firstly, was it the same man? Secondly, why shouldn't he be at an auction? Thirdly, if it was the same man and he was at the auction, it doesn't automatically follow that he killed de Whatshisname.'

Belinda gave a defeated sigh. 'You're right.'

'So do me a favour and forget it. I don't want to hear any more about monks, or for that matter nuns, priests or archbishops.'

With a belligerent look, Hazel turned the car off the road, into a service station and set about refuelling the car. Belinda poked about in the glove box for a caramel but found no comfort, for the packet was empty. She screwed it up and turned to place it in the wastebag, when across the other side of the driveway she saw a small black car pull off the road. It parked nearby. The driver switched off the motor and sat silently at the wheel watching Hazel as she filled the tank. A shiver of fear jolted Belinda as she recognised the driver.

It was the man in the dark suit. The monk.

Hazel hopped from foot to foot like an excited schoolgirl as the recently purchased furniture was unloaded and joined the Chippendale chair in the Wells shop.

Belinda had joined her to assist in the welcoming party but had kept in the background as Hazel fussed over the furniture like a finicky hen fretting over new-laid eggs. She had not told Hazel of her sighting of the monk at the service station, or that he had followed them to Bath.

Belinda had taken the wheel while Hazel dozed for most of the remainder of the journey. The black car had overtaken them several times but always seemed to be waiting further along the highway ready to resume the pursuit. To be honest it was possible, Belinda thought, that the man was simply travelling the same route and it was all a coincidence but even as she thought it, the conviction that he was trailing them grew stronger. It was only on the outskirts of Bath that she had lost sight of the car.

As she moved to assist her friend with the new furniture, Belinda wished that she could ease her mind by confessing her nervousness, but she had no wish to endure another sarcastic put down and silently attempted to shake off her apprehension.

With Belinda's assistance Hazel moved the Georgian table into the prime display space in the window. Apart from the Chippendale chair, the new acquisitions put the other pieces of kitchen furniture in their place and Hazel's pride in her new shop grew apace.

While Hazel busied herself with polishing the table, Belinda was given the task of dusting and attending to the Jacobean cabinet. Set at the back of the shop, it almost filled the width of the small room. Belinda ran her hand over the surface and wondered at the countless other hands that had touched it over the centuries.

Her fingers found the central drawer and she pulled at the handle.

The drawer was stuck fast and it was several minutes before, with much pressure and pushing from side to side, Belinda was able to ease the drawer open. She pulled it towards her and gasped in surprise as she saw the contents.

Fixed firmly in the bottom of the drawer was the framed tapestry with the embroidered image of the crowned king.

'Everything comes to he who waits,' muttered Hazel, in a disbelieving voice. Belinda and Hazel were back at the cottage in Milford. The framed tapestry lay before them on the table as they sipped their afternoon coffee. 'But what I don't understand is how the auctioneers missed it. It must have been in the inventory,' concluded Hazel, with a questioning shrug of her shoulders.

'It wasn't in the catalogue. I looked,' replied Belinda, 'and that surprised me. But if you remember, the day we visited Kidbrooke House, Mr de Montfort put it in the drawer. He was going to repair the glass. It fitted firmly in the drawer and wouldn't have rattled around or made a noise when the cabinet was moved and the drawer was stuck shut very tight, so I imagine no one thought of looking in there. It was simply overlooked.'

Hazel put down her coffee and picked up the frame. She turned it over and with probing fingers began to remove the frail timber backing. 'Judging from the frame, I'd say it was framed in late Victorian times, possibly Edwardian.'

'Do you think the tapestry was made then?'

The backing splintered away and the tapestry slipped from the frame. Hazel shook her head slowly. 'It's certainly older than that.'

'Mr de Montfort said he thought it was seventeenth or eighteenth century.'

'Possibly,' murmured Hazel as her deft fingers explored the fragile linen fabric that lay on the table before them. Folded as it was to fit the frame, it was about a foot square, but both sides had been tucked behind to centre the image of the enthroned king and the top frieze had been folded under. With eager but gentle hands Belinda began to unfold the embroidery. The right side revealed an ornate border of scrolls and flowers as though the work had come to a natural end. The left side when unfolded disclosed something very different. The border was scraggy and uneven as though roughly torn from another piece of fabric. Some of the stitching had come undone and the jagged edge was frayed and tattered.

'It must have been in the frame for a very long time,' whispered Belinda almost reverently. She pointed to the edges of the linen. 'See. The colours are much stronger there where it has been folded away from the light. The centrepiece that was exposed in the frame has faded badly.'

Hazel nodded silently. She seemed strangely withdrawn and pensive. Nevertheless, she began to unfold the top border until it was fully exposed. The colours there were also fresh and Belinda gave a gasp of pleasure as she admired the delicate needlework and the vivid reds, greens, and yellows.

'What do you imagine they represent?' she asked as her fingers traced the outline of the objects disclosed.

'Ecclesiastical stuff, I'd say,' replied Hazel after a pause. 'See, there is a chalice, a cross, and I'm not sure what that is.' She pointed to two circles embroidered in bright saffron coloured stitches. They consisted of one large circle with a smaller one in the centre.

'It looks like a donut,' laughed Belinda. Hazel gave her a censorious glance.

'Hardly. In the seventeenth century?' She inspected the tapestry closely. 'No. They're religious objects. See, there is another type of chalice, or a cup of some sort. A ciborium, I think it's called.'

'What do you think they mean?'

Hazel was silent for a moment as though lost in thought. 'Probably nothing. Probably just decoration. Or they relate to the church the king is sitting in. You know, the divine right of kings and all that. Probably a reminder that he took his vows before God.'

'Well, in that case,' said Belinda, touching the bottom frieze which showed a burial, 'this must show the King's death. Or is it just a reminder of his mortality?'

'But it shows the burial of a monk.' Hazel touched the faded embroidery. 'See, he has a tonsure. The crown of his head is shaved, and William the Conqueror wasn't a monk.'

Belinda took the fabric in her hands and gazed at it wistfully. 'I suppose I'd better hand it back to the auctioneer.' She sighed unconvincingly.

Hazel took the tapestry firmly and laid it back on the table. 'Oh, no you won't. Haven't you heard of the natural law?'

Belinda looked bewildered. 'What natural law?'

'The law of finders keepers. Besides,' said Hazel, as she sat down on the window-seat, 'I paid for it. It was in the drawer of the cabinet I bought, so technically I own it. After all, I didn't put it in the drawer. It was not my fault the auctioneer overlooked it. I bought the cabinet in good faith and if it happens to have contained the tapestry, so what? If there's dust in the drawer I own that as well. Right?'

Belinda nodded her dubious agreement.

'And that being the case, I'm giving the tapestry to you,' concluded Hazel, with a flamboyant gesture worthy of Lady Bountiful.

Belinda's eyes lit up with delight. 'Do you mean it?' she cried, gratefully. 'I really do like it.'

'You're welcome to it,' Hazel smiled benevolently. 'Besides, I find it tatty.' she added disparagingly. But even as she said it, her eyes were drawn to the embroidered linen and a speculative frown mocked her indifference.

The prototypical snowflakes of winter reminded Belinda that Christmas was only five weeks away and she idly wondered how she would spend the festive season. Choosing a warm woollen suit, she prepared herself to meet Mark Sallinger for lunch. Belinda knew that Mark was willing to go beyond their present relationship and propose marriage. But she felt no urgency to embrace matrimony, at least not at the moment, even though she admired Mark's dark good looks and the rugged demeanour that seemed at odds with his public school accent and attitudes. Still, he was an agreeable companion and Belinda was prepared to let the gods plan her future.

The telephone rang just as she was about to switch on the answering machine. Tempted to abandon the caller, she hesitated, but curiosity got the better of her. She picked up the receiver.

'Is that Miss Lawrence? Miss Belinda Lawrence?' The man's voice was deep and demanding. The voice of a man who claimed authority.

'Speaking,' replied Belinda.

'Ah, Miss Lawrence. My name is Godwin. My wife and I are anxious to visit your house and garden. We are great admirers of Capability Brown and understand that your garden has been recently restored to his design.'

'Yes, it has,' replied Belinda, glancing at her watch, 'but I am afraid the house and garden are closed to visitors for the winter. They'll reopen in April.'

There was a silence for a moment at the other end of the phone before the penetrating voice replied. 'I understand, but I wonder if you could make an exception in our case. We have just returned to England after many years abroad and are anxious to catch up with as much sightseeing as possible before the winter curtails our activities.'

Belinda sighed. 'I'm afraid that is not –'

'I know it is an imposition,' the man interrupted, 'but you would be doing us a very great favour and we can be with you in a few minutes. I am calling on the car phone and we're nearby in the next village at Combe Down. We've just been to see the Capability Brown landscape at Prior Park. It would really complete our day if you could do us this favour.'

Belinda silently cursed the man, but she did have time before her luncheon with Mark.

'Very well,' she agreed reluctantly, 'if you can be here quickly, but I am afraid I can only spare a few minutes as I have an appointment.'

'No sooner said than done,' was the reply, 'and my wife and I appreciate your generosity.'

Belinda hung up the phone, switched on the message recorder as protection against any further delays and folded the tapestry into a carrier bag. Mark was knowledgeable about history, and perhaps he could shed some light on its origins.

True to his word the man and his wife arrived within five minutes. Belinda opened the door to an impressive man of about fifty. A well-preserved fifty, with tanned skin and sleek dark hair just turning interestingly grey. He was well dressed and his dark brown eyes possessed an intelligent gleam. All in all he was a charismatic and powerful figure. He also exuded an ambiguous charm.

'Miss Lawrence?' He took Belinda's hand in a firm grip. 'May I introduce myself. I'm Charles Godwin. This is very kind of you to put yourself out. May I introduce my wife?' Belinda turned to the woman who accompanied him. Mrs Godwin was about thirty-five. She was plainly dressed, almost drab, thought Belinda. But her eyes were watchful and although not beautiful, she was attractive with long blonde hair drawn back severely off her face and cascading down her back in a ponytail. She nodded her silent introduction to Belinda.

'If you will allow us a few moments to photograph the garden,' said Mr Godwin, producing a camera, 'we will be on our way.'

Taking his wife by the elbow, he led her down into the garden. Belinda stood at the window and watched the couple as Mr Godwin snapped photo after photo. It seemed to her that he was indiscriminate in his selection of subjects and just pointing wildly and shooting whatever came into his viewfinder without any regard for what he photographed.

As she watched, Belinda became aware that Mrs Godwin's attention was not on the garden. She was staring intently back at the house. Mr Godwin put his camera back in its case, the two visitors conversed briefly, then made their way back to the front door. Belinda gathered her bag and prepared to farewell them.

Mr Godwin stepped resolutely into the hall. 'I wonder if we could impose upon your generosity for another moment and take a brief look at your house.'

Without waiting for Belinda's reply the two strode into the hall and proceeded into the main sitting room. Mrs Godwin ran her hand over the back of a chair. 'You have some fine pieces here,' she said in a surprisingly masculine voice, 'did you inherit them along with the property?'

'I'm afraid not,' replied Belinda tersely, irritated now by the delay caused by the visitors. 'Most of the furniture here belongs to my business partner, Mrs Whitby.'

Husband and wife exchanged a swift glance. 'Would that be the Mrs Whitby who has the antique shop on Pulteney Bridge?' Mr Godwin asked, as though he knew the answer and posed the question purely as a formality.

'That's right,' retorted Belinda in a tight voice.

'She certainly knows her subject,' said Mrs Godwin admiringly, as she moved about the room touching the furniture as though conveying her approval. 'Has she bought anything recently? For instance, did she attend the auction at Kidbrooke House in Yorkshire?'

Belinda looked at the woman in amazement.

'The reason I ask,' continued Mrs Godwin hurriedly, 'is that we wanted to attend but were delayed and unable to get there.'

'We understand that there were some fine pieces auctioned and as we're refurbishing our new home we are anxious to obtain the best we can,' added Mr Godwin, with a censorious glance at his wife. 'I spent many years in Yorkshire as a younger man and got to know Kidbrooke House intimately. I always admired it and envied the owner.'

'Are any of these pieces from Kidbrooke House?' asked Mrs Godwin, looking Belinda directly in the eye.

Belinda felt a wave of distaste for the Godwins, and shook her head. 'The few pieces that Mrs Whitby purchased are at her shop in Wells. You'd have to contact her and make an appointment to view them. Otherwise the shop is open each market day.'

'And what day would that be?' probed Mrs Godwin belligerently.

Belinda ignored the question and glanced ostentatiously at her watch. 'Now if you don't mind, I must ask you to leave. I am already late for an appointment.' She led the way to the front door and stood by as the couple stepped out onto the terrace.

'Thank you once again, Miss Lawrence,' said Mr Godwin turning to Belinda. 'You have been very helpful,' he added in an impassive voice.

Mrs Godwin nodded a cold acknowledgement and the two turned and walked to the garden gate. From her vantage point at the front door, Belinda watched them as they walked to their car. At their approach the driver stepped out and opened the passenger door for them.

With a shock, Belinda saw that it was a young man with shaved hair.

'Monks?' questioned Mark, as he poured coffee. He carried the cups to the sofa where Belinda sat smoothing the tapestry carefully on her lap.

'Well, they were wearing monks' habits and had short hair.'

Mark sank onto the sofa beside her. The luncheon had been excellent, confirming Belinda's suspicions that Mark was a superb cook. She silently admired his handsome features and ran an appreciative eye over his muscular frame covered now by impeccable English tailoring. With his wide knowledge of wines, food, politics, architecture and history, he was the ideal man. Perhaps she was being obtuse in deferring any permanent liaison with him. However …?

Sinking back she gave a sigh, not of fulfilment but of frustration.

'It seems everywhere I go now I see these young blokes with close cropped or shaven hair,' she continued, 'even in Milford.'

'Well in some quarters it's fashionable to shave one's head.' Mark ran his fingers through his own voluptuous dark hair.

Or perhaps they are *monks*, thought Belinda. Aloud she said, 'But that's not what I want to talk about.' She held out the tapestry. 'What do you make of this?'

Mark took the fabric and inspected it. 'Where did you get it?'

Belinda gave a brief résumé of the acquisition of the tapestry and William de Montfort's murder. 'But what I want to know is, how old is it and it is of any value?' she concluded.

Mark rose and took a large volume from the bookcase that lined one wall of the room. He flipped open the pages and laid it on the sofa beside Belinda. 'This is a detailed photographic illustration of the Bayeux Tapestry made a few years ago when it was being cleaned. It's full size and shows all the details.'

'I saw the Victorian copy at Reading,' murmured Belinda, her attention taken with the glowing photographs.

Mark was examining the fragment of tapestry by the light of the window. 'This is certainly very old. But it doesn't correspond to any part of the Bayeux original that I can recall. That ends with the defeat of the English at the hands of the invading Normans. It stops short of showing William being crowned king. Not like this.'

Belinda glanced up from the book. 'Hazel thinks it was framed in Victorian times but the embroidery could be seventeenth century.'

Mark shook his head. 'Not likely. If it's an attempt to copy or imitate the original, it is highly unlikely that it'd have been done then. Mediaeval art was not popular at that time, at least not in England and the Tapestry itself was really only brought to prominence in France in the early part of the eighteenth century. Of course, it is possible that your tapestry was made in France or another European country but there's something about it that suggests it's older. Of course it could be a near contemporary of the original, made in similar style. Probably a fragment of some wall hanging.'

'Where was the original made? Wasn't it in France?'

Mark put the linen fragment down and sat next to Belinda. 'People thought so for years, but there seems to be some evidence now that it was made here in England.'

Belinda pointed to the frieze of church objects and the one below showing the funeral of a monk. 'And what about these? Do you think they've any meaning?'

'In the Bayeux Tapestry the borders certainly comment upon the main story in one form or another.'

'So these religious things could have some bearing on the coronation of King William?'

Mark shrugged. 'I doubt it. They are probably just decorative.'

But that doesn't explain the corpse on the bottom border, thought Belinda.

'Still, if you're serious about getting a full explanation,' continued Mark, looking at his watch and rising, 'why not have a chat with your local Vicar?'

'The Vicar?' Belinda looked bewildered.

'Yes. He's a bit of an expert on mediaeval history and certainly knows more than I do.' Mark pulled on his coat. 'I'd better be off. I've got some clients waiting for me in Bathampton. They're inspecting a property and my commission is a healthy one.' He hesitated at the door. 'Had any more phone calls from Australia?'

Belinda smiled to herself. 'Only my mother.'

Mark gave an unbelieving grunt.

Belinda folded the tapestry scrap away and picked up the book on the Bayeux Tapestry. 'Do you mind if I borrow this?'

'Not at all. And don't forget to give the Vicar a call.'

As Belinda drove home from Bath she made a mental note to contact the Reverend Lawson. He had officiated at the funeral of her great aunt Jane and over the last year she had got to know the elderly man quite well. His wife had died several years ago and he managed the small parish well enough by himself. There were few parishioners these days, and on the infrequent Sunday morning visits that Belinda made to the church, it seemed that the congregation shrank on each occasion.

The church itself was tiny and dated from the sixteenth century, although there was evidence of Saxon origins in the foundations. Reverend Lawson had been a regular visitor to her cottage during the time that Belinda was renovating the garden and his enthusiasm buoyed her up in her moments of anxiety over the wisdom of what she was doing. She decided that she would invite him for Sunday lunch after morning service. He was partial to roast lamb, she knew, and the stickier the pudding the better. Gorged with a Sabbath banquet he would no doubt fall into a bucolic frame of mind and she would be able to entice him into divulging his knowledge of the Bayeux Tapestry and, hopefully, her own scrap of embroidery. That is, if he didn't fall asleep in front of the fire.

No time like the present. She would be passing the Vicarage on the way home, so she might as well call in and offer the invitation now. As she turned off the main road in the direction of the church, she dialled her home number on her mobile phone and keyed in the code number to activate her message machine.

Hazel Whitby's distraught voice hissed from the earpiece. 'Bel, give me a call as soon as you come in. Some bastard has broken into the shop in Wells. I'm here now with the police and I'll wait until I hear from you.'

With a U-turn that surprised her with its severity, Belinda swung the car around between two opposing gateways that led into fields and sped off back along the narrow country lane, hoping against hope that there was no vehicle approaching from the other direction.

Her guardian angel had obviously travelled with her on the journey for she arrived in record time, just as the police car departed from Hazel's shop. Hazel herself stood in the doorway, her mouth set in a grim straight line.

'Can you believe it?' she demanded of Belinda as she approached the shop. 'In broad daylight?'

Belinda forced herself to breathe deeply and calm her strained nerves. 'How did they get in?'

Hazel led the way into the shop and gestured towards the back room. 'Smashed the window at the back and climbed in. I still hadn't got the alarm installed. It was due tomorrow, can you believe? God knows what the insurance boys will say.'

Belinda looked around the room. Nothing appeared disturbed and everything was as they had left it after the arrival of the furniture from York. 'Well, at least they didn't take anything or do any damage.'

Hazel gave her a murderous look. 'Oh, really?' she demanded, her voice pure acid. She walked to the Georgian table installed in the window. 'What would you call that?'

Belinda glanced down at the table and gave a small cry of horror.

Etched deeply into the dark wood was an enigmatic inscription, carved violently by a savage hand wielding a razor sharp instrument: HAROLD REX INTERFECTUS EST.

Three

'King Harold was killed.'

'What in the hell are you talking about?' Hazel was in no mood for violent accusations, especially cryptic historical ones.

'That's what it means,' snapped Belinda. 'It's a quotation from the Bayeux Tapestry.'

Hazel took a deep swig of her gin and tonic. The two women had repaired to the Star and Swan to calm their nerves and to contemplate the meaning of what, on the surface, was a senseless act of vandalism.

The book of the Bayeux Tapestry Belinda had borrowed from Mark lay open on the table before them. 'See.' Belinda tapped the page with her finger. The Latin text inscribed on the tapestry was translated in English below. Belinda read it out again, as though explaining to a child. 'It translates as "King Harold was killed", and the illustration shows King Harold being slain in battle and the Normans looting the English dead.'

Hazel fidgeted angrily. 'Belinda. I've no doubt it does. I don't question that. All I want to know is – why did they carve it on my table? My very *expensive* table?'

Belinda had no idea why, and thought silence the better part of valour until Hazel had got over her hostility.

'I mean,' continued Hazel, obviously not expecting an answer to her questions, just a sympathetic ear, 'if they had to scrawl graffiti on something, why not the walls? At least I could paint over them. But to do irreparable damage to that gorgeous table is beyond the pale.'

Belinda nodded a mute agreement and the two sat in offended silence. Belinda was as confused as Hazel, and her mind began to wander along various avenues in an attempt to find a rational explanation. It seemed unlikely that the average burglar would go to the trouble of carving Latin quotations on furniture as a way of venting his spleen on not finding anything he considered valuable. And that was the odd thing. Apart from the damage to the table, nothing was missing and no harm done to other objects. It also seemed strange the break in had taken place after the arrival of the furniture from Kidbrooke House. Stranger still that the Latin inscription carved in the tabletop should come from the Bayeux Tapestry and she should have a portion of a tapestry that bore a resemblance to that historical work.

The thought of Kidbrooke House stirred another memory of a recent event and Belinda turned to her companion who had returned from the bar with a fresh supply of "mother's ruin".

'By the way,' Belinda asked, as Hazel sank dejectedly into her seat, 'did you get a phone call from someone wanting to look over your furniture?'

Hazel shook her head dispiritedly. 'No. When?'

'Earlier today. Are you sure? Because something odd happened this morning, just as I was about to leave to have lunch with Mark. A man and his wife rang and practically forced their way in to look over the house and garden.'

'Then why would they ring me?' asked Hazel, reaching for her drink.

'Well, the peculiar thing was that they seemed more interested in the house and the furnishings than the garden, although it was the garden they said they wanted to see, Capability Brown and all that. The woman seemed anxious to know if any of the furniture came from Kidbrooke House.'

Hazel showed more interest. 'Why would she ask that?'

'That's what I wondered,' replied Belinda, 'except that he, the husband, said that he knew Kidbrooke House from years ago and had missed the auction and was keen to purchase some of the objects from the house. And that's what I thought rather strange.'

'What?'

'That he should think there would be any of the furniture in my house. Unless ...'

'Unless he knew that we were at the auction.'

The two women looked at each other.

'How would he know that?'

Hazel toyed with her already half empty glass. 'He could have found out from the auctioneer.'

Belinda considered this. 'Yes. I suppose that's how he knew.' But she was not convinced. 'Anyway, I told them that you had some of the furniture for sale here in Wells and that they should ring you and make a time to look it over. And you say he didn't ring you?'

'Don't remember them,' shrugged Hazel. 'What's their name? This couple?'

'Er ... Godfrey? No ... Godwin.'

There was a brief silence as the two sipped their drinks.

'Hazel?' said Belinda, contemplatively, 'has it occurred to you that there may be some connection between the bit of tapestry from Kidbrooke House and the Latin quotation carved on your table?'

Hazel took a deep breath before she replied. And when she did her voice betrayed a surprising nervousness. 'Yes. I'm certain of it. I didn't like to say anything before, because you like that damned thing so much, but it gives me the shivers. It has an air of death about it and I wish to God you'd get rid of it.'

Belinda looked at her companion in amazement. 'Oh, Hazel. You're going a bit far aren't you? It's only a scrap of linen. What harm can it do?'

Hazel rubbed her arms apprehensively. 'If I knew that, I'd tell you. All I ask is that you keep it out of sight. Keep it locked away safely so no one can find it. Believe me, it'll bring bad luck.'

As she drove back home, Belinda recalled Hazel's prediction and remembered her own initial uneasiness about the tapestry.

'Stuff and nonsense,' she chided herself. 'How can a scrap of fabric bring bad luck?'

But nevertheless, the mysterious connection between it and both the Bayeux Tapestry and the inscription carved on the table-top intrigued her.

'I only hope Reverend Lawson can provide an answer,' she muttered as she turned off the highway towards the village of Milford.

'They were bloody times, indiscriminate slaughter and violent rape were the order of the day.' The Reverend Lawson sounded almost nostalgic for things past as he patted his snow-white hair and took his place at Belinda's table.

'Not unlike life today,' commented Belinda, punctuating her remark by wielding a sharp carving knife.

The Sunday Communion service had been sparsely attended but even the Vicar had to admit that the prospect of sitting in the frigid church, now that winter chills permeated the stone walls, sorely tested Christian discipline. His rheumatism was particularly bad this year and seemed to increase in intensity as each new winter approached, while climbing into the pulpit each week had become a debatable penance in itself. Indeed, if he were to be honest with himself, he would have admitted it was the prospect of roast lamb and a deliciously sticky pudding that had got him through the frustrating ceremony.

Reverend Lawson settled his rotund frame firmly in his chair and watched hungrily as Belinda began to carve the roast lamb.

'Of course, your little piece of tapestry is intriguing,' he said, wrenching his glance from the meat to the embroidery he smoothed on the tabletop. 'I must say that the style is remarkably similar to *La Tapissérie de la Reine Mathilde.*'

Belinda paused in her carving, causing the pink-faced cleric to glance apprehensively at the meat, fearing some disastrous delay in the arrival of his meal. 'Remarkably similar to what?' she asked.

Reverend Lawson's mouth watered at the sight of the succulent juices flowing from the perfectly cooked lamb. 'That was the traditional name for the Bayeux Tapestry. It springs from the ancient belief that Queen Matilda, the conqueror's queen, personally embroidered the work.'

Belinda resumed her carving, to an audible relieved sigh from the clergyman. 'Did she?'

'The origins of the work are obscure but there is some evidence that it was commissioned by Odo. Odo was the half-brother of William the Conqueror and was bishop of Bayeux.'

The delectable meat was placed before him and he helped himself generously to the baked vegetables and green peas.

'So it was an act of brotherly love? To honour him? He had it made to record his brother's success?' suggested Belinda as she helped herself to the meat.

'Odo had much to be thankful for,' said the Reverend, lavishing mint sauce upon his repast. 'He was only thirteen years old when William, the older and powerful brother, handed him the bishopric, so he quickly became involved in ecclesiastical and political affairs.'

'He was involved in politics as well?'

'The Norman invasion of England in 1066 expanded his horizon and he certainly took part in planning the conquest. His activities portrayed in the Bayeux Tapestry may be exaggerated but after William was crowned king, Odo was given Dover castle and created Earl of Kent. And that was no easy task. Canterbury was a defiant region still rankling over the invader's triumph.'

'So there was opposition to Odo?' asked Belinda, as she again passed the vegetable dish to Reverend Lawson. He took a third crisp roast potato. A large one.

'Very much so. He was disliked because he took possession of most of the land and in some cases, land that belonged to the church. He was also accused of robbing the churches and abbeys of their treasures. Archbishop Lanfranc, the archbishop of Canterbury, took Odo to court in an attempt to regain some of the church's estates.'

The Vicar took time off to devote his energies noisily to his meal. After several moments Belinda, fearing he would loose his train of thought, felt it necessary to prompt him.

'So his production of the Tapestry was not only to praise his brother William's achievements, but to glorify himself? To make a big man of himself?'

'Yes. On various occasions when the king was absent from England, Odo was vice-regent. But he must have displeased the king in some way, because William, for reasons unclear to us, had Odo imprisoned. Some say it was because he fancied himself as Pope. Whatever the reason, Odo claimed immunity because he was a bishop and therefore outside the control of the law, but William sneakily replied, "I am not arresting the bishop of Bayeux. I arrest the Earl of Kent", and that put paid to Odo's freedom.'

With a satisfied sigh, the cleric lay down his knife and fork. Belinda smiled and gathered the empty dishes, only to return from the kitchen with a steaming date pudding engulfed by a rich chocolate sauce. It was accompanied by a bowl of clotted cream and the old man's eyes glazed as the dessert was spooned into his bowl.

'It seems to me,' said Belinda, as she dropped an extra dollop of cream onto the dish, 'that if Odo had the tapestry made it was to curry favour with his brother. But if he spent most of his life in England after the conquest, why have it made in France?'

'Not sure that he did,' slurred the Vicar, through the chocolate sauce, 'there is every chance it was made here in England.'

'Where?

'Some say Winchester. Others plump for Canterbury. But wherever it was made it is our only contemporary or near contemporary record of the events surrounding the conquest. It was made somewhere between 1070 and 1080.'

'You don't think it would favour the Norman version of events?'

'Oh, undoubtedly. But it does record the main occurrences. Such as the events leading up to the invasion and the slaughter of the claimant to the English throne, Harold Godwinson, at the Battle of Hastings.'

Belinda paused with her spoon poised halfway between bowl and mouth.

'Harold who?'

'Godwinson. Harold was the son of Earl Godwin and brother to Edward the Confessor's wife.'

'But that's extraordinary!' cried Belinda.

'How so?' asked the Reverend, scraping up the last of the cream and chocolate sauce.

'But only the other day I met someone by that name. Godwin. It's such an unusual name.'

'Be that as it may, my dear, it was the family name of Harold Godwinson, the King of England.'

Belinda leant back in her chair, her eyes bright with suspicion. 'And King Harold was killed,' she said softly, the legend carved in Hazel's tabletop springing clearly into her mind.

Reverend Lawson pulled on his heavy overcoat and plunged his plump fingers into warm gloves. 'If you trust me, my dear, I may be able to assist you in dating your piece of tapestry.'

Belinda paused in wrapping a small bunch of flowers that she intended to place on her great aunt Jane's grave in the nearby churchyard. 'That'd be great. But how?'

'It would necessitate sending it away, I'm afraid.'

'Oh. I'm not sure I'd like that,' Belinda replied hesitantly, 'but if you think it ...'

The old man nodded. 'I know what you mean. But an erstwhile acquaintance, actually an extremely old friend – we were at university together – is very much an expert in this field. He knows about tapestry and mediaeval things, things like iconography and the interpretation of manuscripts and if anyone can put a date on it, he can. He lives in Winchester and I'm sure that if I sent it to him he would give me an accurate report.'

Belinda frowned. 'I wouldn't feel happy just sending it off by mail.'

Reverend Lawson spread his wool-encased hands in agreement. 'I understand what you mean. Perhaps … perhaps I could take it personally.' He looked suddenly cheerful. 'I could get a few days off before the Christmas rush; indeed, I would welcome it. And it would give me great pleasure to see Gerald again.'

'Gerald?' enquired Belinda, as she slipped into her overcoat.

'Hmmm. Gerald Taylor. *Sir* Gerald Taylor, actually. My friend from academia. If I were to take the tapestry with me I could get the report first hand.'

'Wouldn't that be too much trouble?'

'Oh, no.' The Reverend waved away such a foolish suggestion. 'To tell the truth, it would provide me with much-needed mental stimulation.' He dropped his voice as though not wishing to offend the parish. 'There is little here in Milford, other than the occasional funeral, that provides a challenge so to speak, and they are decreasing in number as the congregation diminishes, so I would welcome this melodrama.'

Belinda wondered just how challenging a funeral could be. 'Well, if I can't trust a clergyman, who can I trust?' She smiled at Reverend Lawson and handed the scrap of tapestry to him. The parson took the fabric gently and, folding it carefully, slipped it into his coat pocket.

'Don't you worry, my dear, I shall guard it with my life.'

Locking the door behind her, Belinda joined Reverend Lawson on his afternoon stroll back to the Vicarage. The sun had emerged from its cloudy lair and though the air was chill it was not an unpleasant ramble along the country lanes.

As they reached the churchyard, Belinda saw a figure sauntering through the ancient tombs on the far side of the graveyard. The person, as though sensing their arrival and wishing solitude, blended into the shadows of the overhanging trees and disappeared from sight. It was probably a visitor to the village filling in a few minutes browsing in the old cemetery and amusing themselves by reading the verbose memorial texts on the flamboyant headstones. Yet Belinda felt a moment of unease.

They stopped at aunt Jane's grave and Belinda rested the spray of flowers on top of the marble memorial. She said a silent prayer for her aunt's peace of spirit and stepped back to join Reverend Lawson who was waiting a step behind, a suitably pious expression on his face, which masked the severe attack of dyspepsia he was experiencing from overindulging in the pleasures of sticky pudding.

'Tell me, Vicar,' said Belinda, surreptitiously scraping some cloying mud from her shoe, 'are there any monasteries nearby?'

'Monasteries?' The clergyman looked bewildered, as though he had heard the word for the first time.

'Yes, you know, nuns or monks?'

Reverend Lawson shivered with the cold and shook his head. 'No, I am sorry to say, the days of monasteries seem doomed. There are so few embracing the religious life these days. And those that do ... well ...' He left Belinda to interpret his feelings on the newly ordained.

'So there are no monks at all?'

'Yes, there are some, but not in this area. There was once a Carthusian priory at Hinton Charterhouse but that has long gone.'

'Because I saw some only recently. Very young men in grey robes and with very short hair. I thought they seemed extremely young to have given their life to God.'

'You can never be too young for that,' reprimanded the Vicar sententiously. He wrinkled his brow in thought. 'Did you say a grey habit?'

Belinda nodded.

'Well, I would hardly call them monks,' the man said censoriously, 'but I believe that there is a so-called "religious community" on the outskirts of Norton St Philip. They're much given to bells and smells and meditating. I gather they have attracted some of the more gullible youths from hereabouts and they have fashioned themselves some sort of habit, which I believe is grey. Much given to the veneration of St Augustine.'

'Is it a monastery?'

'Hardly. I gather they have taken over an old farmstead. Self-sufficiency and all that hippie attitude. Communal living and grubby feet combined with ambiguous sanctimonious claptrap.'

'Perhaps they feel happy worshipping that way?'

Reverend Lawson snorted his disbelief.

'But they just can't have formed this group by themselves,' continued Belinda, 'I mean the young people. Have they got a leader?'

The Vicar rubbed his brow. 'I did hear their name. Strange husband and wife team. He's charismatic – that fashionable word – she's earthy. A mother figure. They chant mumbo jumbo and the children are fascinated. Promise to give up their worldly goods etcetera. Now what was their name? I should know it, because I was only discussing them with Mrs Darby the other day while she was doing the altar flowers. Her sister lives in Norton St Philip and is scandalised by the presence of the so-called monks in the main street. Also, there have been reports of a few of the monks misbehaving in the George Inn and the presence of police, to quieten the rowdy lads, has been called for. Mrs Darby was full of the group's activities, so I should remember the name of the couple who led them.'

His brow wrinkled with the effort. Suddenly his forehead cleared and a smile of wonderment lit his face.

'Well, I'll be blessed. If that isn't a strange thing?'

Belinda waited for an explanation. When it was not forthcoming she felt the need to ask. 'What's so strange?'

The Vicar turned and looked at her. 'We mentioned the name only a short time ago. How remarkable that it should arise again.'

Belinda frowned in exasperation. 'Well? What is it?'

'The name of the English king. Godwin.'

'As you have to take Rusty back to Norton St Philip today, let's leave early and I'll buy you lunch at the George.'

Rusty was Mark Sallinger's extra large, extra boisterous dog, which he had bought on the spur of the moment and realised, after losing a priceless vase and sustaining serious damage to his furniture, was too big to keep in his small house. Rusty was boarded out in a farm at nearby Norton St Philip and came home to share Mark's weekends.

It was the Sunday following the Reverend Lawson's banquet and the capricious winter had suddenly turned on a delightful sunny day that tempted the residents of Bath from their cosy firesides. Belinda and Mark, accompanied by the extroverted Rusty, had joined the promenade and spent the morning browsing in antique and book shops and now, after a refreshing cup of coffee, were climbing the hill to Mark's house.

'You're remarkably free with your money,' joked Mark in reply to Belinda's offer to buy lunch.

'Don't worry,' smiled Belinda, 'it'll only be a Ploughman's.' She slipped her arm though Mark's. 'Tell me. Do you know anything about the religious community at Norton St Philip?'

Mark looked askance. 'You mean the Holy Rollers?'

'Do I? I'm not sure what they call themselves.'

'That's what the locals call them. Wandering around in their grey robes chanting phoney Gregorian chants.'

'Grey robes!' exclaimed Belinda. 'Yes, that sounds like them. With short or shaved hair?'

'Only the fellows,' replied Mark, 'the women, if you can call them that, have long greasy hair that looks as though it needs a good wash. In fact, they all look as though they could do with a hot bath.' He looked suspiciously at Belinda. 'Why do you want to know? Are you thinking of joining them?'

Belinda gave him an amused punch on the arm. 'Can you see me wandering through the streets chanting hymns?'

Mark smiled. 'I wouldn't be surprised at anything you did.'

They had reached the tiny garden in front of Mark's house. The dog scampered across the street, indicating that he at least was not prepared to go indoors just yet. Belinda leant against the fence.

'Have you ever seen the people who run the community?'

Mark shook his head.

'I've met them,' said Belinda. Mark turned to her.

'Where?'

'They came to look over the garden at Milford one day. Their name is Godwin. Does that name mean anything to you?'

'Can't say that it does. Other than Mary Shelley.'

'Mary Shelley? How does she come into it?'

'I seem to remember telling you this once before,' gibed Mark. 'Godwin was her maiden name. Mary Godwin.'

Belinda looked thoughtful and turned to enter the garden. 'Oh yes – *Frankenstein*. No,' she said as she walked up the path to the front door, 'I don't mean her. I mean the founders of the Holy Rollers. I just thought that you might have heard of them. I don't think they've been in the area for long and people around here seem suspicious of newcomers. I thought there might have been talk about them, that's all.'

Mark ushered a reluctant Rusty into the garden and closed the front gate. 'Well, as you seem so curious about them and their brotherhood we can drive by the commune and you can check them out. That is, after the lunch you promised me.'

The Reverend Lawson settled himself comfortably in the coach seat and opened a newly purchased packet of chewy mints. The prospect of a week on holiday filled him with satisfaction. The bus bound for Winchester had few passengers.

Much like this morning's Communion Service, thought the clergyman resentfully. His dwindling congregation depressed him but he could think of nothing that would induce the villagers to worship. That desire had to come from the parishioners themselves.

The portly man put these depressing thoughts from his mind and instead concentrated on the cheerful prospect of seeing his old friend, Sir Gerald. The fragment of tapestry was secure in his overnight bag resting on the empty seat beside him. If anyone could provide information as to its origin, Sir Gerald could.

The driver took his place behind the wheel and Reverend Lawson squirmed comfortably in his seat. A trip through the beautiful English countryside on such a sunny day was the ideal panacea for his religious worries. It reminded him of the far-off days of his youth and the red-letter holidays when he, and his youthful companions, had taken charabanc trips to the Lake District and picnicked by Lake Windermere. He had proposed to his wife at Orrest Head, where the lake spread out before them like a giant blue mirror. The distant memory brought a wistful mist to his eyes.

As the door to the bus swung shut two young people, a boy and a girl, both waving tickets, ran eagerly from the booking desk. The driver reopened the door to allow the two latecomers on board.

Reverend Lawson looked disapprovingly at the grubby couple as they scrambled up the steps. The girl, who couldn't have been more than sixteen, looked like a gypsy with scarves and bangles while the boy, probably about eighteen, wore torn jeans and his hair was shorn very short. In his ear he wore an earring from which dangled a small silver cross.

The Reverend frowned at this sacrilege and watched

disapprovingly as the two made their way down the aisle. As they drew level the two latecomers leered at him and burst into mocking giggles. Reverend Lawson's cherub-pink face blushed red with indignation and he turned his gaze out of the window. The boy and girl proceeded down to the rear of the bus and collapsed in a further outburst of sniggers.

The elderly man, feeling he was the butt of their amusement, was tight with rage. He was angry that they had spoilt his enjoyment of the coming journey and hoped that the annoying children would leave the bus at the first stop and not continue all the way to Winchester.

The unexpected sunshine had made lunching in the galleried courtyard at the George Inn irresistible and the planned Ploughman's Lunch had given way, under the onslaught of a tantalising aroma, to a tasty ragoût washed down with a very pleasant drop of red.

'I'm afraid this has cost you more than the ten shillings it cost Samuel Pepys when he dined here in 1668,' muttered Mark, through a mouthful of deliciously tender beef.

Belinda smiled contentedly. 'I'm sure it wouldn't be a complete meal without you dredging up some historical reference.'

Mark took mock offence. 'Well, it's perfectly true. Pepys ate here with his wife – who was born in Somerset, by the way – when they were on a trip to Bath. They stopped in Norton St Philip, had a meal and then Sam visited the grave of the fair maids of Fosscott.'

Belinda put down her empty wineglass and turned a jaundiced eye on Mark. 'Fair maids of what?'

Mark mopped up the remaining gravy with his bread. 'Two women from hereabouts. Joined at the belly since birth.'

'Siamese twins.'

'You *are* perceptive,' said Mark as he swallowed the last of his meal and swilled it down with the remains of the wine.

'Perceptive and curious, but not about Siamese twins or Samuel Pepys. What interests me is the farm run by the "Holy Rollers." You said we could take a look at it, so …'

'So let's do just that,' cried Mark, as he threw down his napkin and leapt to his feet. 'That is, after you've paid the bill. You know, I believe that I could get used to being a kept man.'

'Well, don't hold your breath,' grinned Belinda as they made their way inside the hotel.

The car park was full, due to the number of enthusiastic diners lured by the clement weather and the fine food at the inn, so that it was some minutes before Mark could extricate his car from the parking bay. A short distance past the hotel he turned off into a country lane and proceeded on for another mile. The lane was deserted but Mark drove with caution as the narrow path twisted and turned sharply and high hedgerows limited his vision.

As he turned a corner, he was forced to brake sharply to avoid hitting a youth ambling along the middle of the road towards Norton St Philip.

Mark muttered an obscene curse under his breath. The jeans and T-shirt clad youth, who appeared to be in no hurry to step aside, ambled across to the car window. He peered belligerently into the car.

Belinda gave a gasp. It was one of the monks from Kidbrooke House.

'Sorry, old chap,' called Mark, in unconvincing tones that clearly conveyed the wish that perhaps he had run the brat down.

The young man sneered his reply and with a thump of his fist hit the top of Mark's car before he slid past and resumed his walk.

'Cheeky beggar,' snapped Mark, watching him in the rear vision mirror.

'Mark. He's one of the monks.' Belinda craned her neck to watch the shorthaired youth depart. Mark accelerated the car and they continued down the lane.

'Didn't look like a monk to me,' he snapped. 'More like a member of the Hitler Youth.'

Belinda sat back in her seat and faced the road. 'I know what you mean. Still, I'm certain I saw him at Kidbrooke House the day William de Montfort was murdered. There were two of them. And I saw the other one again at the auction.'

Mark gave her a curious look. 'You don't think he's connected with the murder?'

Belinda looked out the window at the passing fields. 'I'm not sure,' she replied uncertainly.

They drove on in silence for a few more minutes until Mark pulled over to the side of the road and switched off the engine.

They were on the brow of a hill and sloping away from them was a small farm. The thatched farmhouse lay towards the bottom of the hill near a small stream. It was an idyllic picture of rural England with cattle and sheep grazing. Fowls scratched for food and there were fields green with vegetables. Other than a few distant figures working in the fields, the place appeared deserted.

Mark pointed to a sign that hung above the gateway entrance to the farm. In Gothic lettering it read: *The Fellowship of St Augustine.*

A faint foreign sound intruded into the peaceful natural sounds of the Sunday afternoon.

'What's that noise?' asked Belinda, straining her ears to catch the sound. Mark peered through the windscreen and pointed towards the farmhouse.

Behind the building and from the direction of the brook came a procession of people. Some were dressed in the grey habits of monks, others in normal dress. At the head of the parade was a monk carrying a crude wooden cross. Behind him came a boy waving an incense burner and leading three young women in long white robes. The girls each had a coronet of green leaves on their heads. The remainder of the monks and attendants followed and they all gave voice to a Gregorian chant.

Belinda watched in amazement. Then her eyes grew wide with astonishment. Taking up the rear of the procession were two figures cloaked in gold capes.

'It's them,' Belinda cried. 'It's the Godwins.'

Reverend Lawson made his way past Winchester Cathedral. The bus had deposited him safely at his destination and his indignation towards the troublesome young passengers dissipated although he had kept a wary eye upon them. He was relieved when, after the bus had drawn to a halt, they had pushed past the remaining travellers and, with an impressive display of immature animation, left the bus before disappearing into the evening mists.

The unpretentious facade of the Cathedral loomed above the vicar, but in his mind's eye he recalled its cavernous interior and made a mental note to revisit it at the first opportunity.

A remembered image of the mortuary chests located above the choir screens and reputed to have contained the remains of Anglo-Saxon kings brought to mind the justification of his visit to Winchester.

Pulling his coat close across his chest against any chill the night might offer, he clutched tightly at the bag containing the mysterious tapestry with the stitched image of William the Conqueror. He was eager to display it for Sir Gerald and anticipated many pleasurable moments in the forthcoming week as the two relived old times and pontificated on the origins of the embroidered work.

As he stepped from the shadows of the cathedral and hurried down Kingsgate Street to Sir Gerald's house he was aware of activity somewhere behind him. Loud laughter and ribald comment that sounded familiar unnerved him and caused him to increase his stride. Through the congealing mist Sir Gerald's house appeared before him and with relief, he hurried up the steps, rang the bell and waited to be admitted.

The insidious sniggering continued and he glanced over his shoulder. A streetlight switched on and beneath its glow he saw the young boy and girl, his aggravating travelling companions. They seemed consumed with each other and ignored him. He could smell the sour tang of chips and the greasy nauseating odour of hamburger.

To his relief, the door to the house was opened and he was admitted to its warmth and protection. The two young travellers seemed oblivious to his departure and continued feeding each other the unsavoury cuisine.

However, their laughter ceased and as the door closed behind Reverend Lawson they became silent and watchful. In the still Wessex night they were the only signs of human life in the now dark and deserted street.

The following week passed uneventfully for Belinda. Hazel Whitby had taken off to some auction sales in Cornwall and Belinda had been left in charge of the shop in Bath. With the seasonal decline of the tourists there had been little to do and the few customers who entered the shop had browsed rather than bought, so that towards week's end Belinda had taken to closing the shop mid-afternoon. In the time she spent seated behind the counter, watching the passing parade over Pulteney Bridge, her thoughts recycled the events of the past few weeks. Her intuition told her that there was some connection between the murder of William de Montfort and the Fellowship of St Augustine. But what was the connection? Other than the conviction that two of the so-called monks had been at Kidbrooke House on the day of the murder, and that was a very tenuous link, there was nothing she could demonstrate that supported her belief. Mark had pooh-poohed her hunch and Hazel had seemed distracted and refused to indulge her whenever Belinda raised the subject. But the Godwins *had* expressed interest in purchasing furniture from Kidbrooke

House and they were the creators of the Fellowship of St Augustine.

And there was the coincidence, if it was a coincidence, of the Latin inscription carved in the tabletop. An inscription taken from the Bayeux Tapestry. And the tapestry that came from Kidbrooke House matched the style of that great work. Coincidence again? Belinda was not convinced.

On the Friday afternoon, Belinda had driven out to Norton St Philip and parked the car at the top of the hill. Below her, in the late afternoon gloom, the farm lay grey and colourless. There was nothing that looked out of the ordinary. For all intents and purposes it could have been any farm in England. One or two figures worked in the fields while another rounded up the cows for milking. Belinda turned the car around and drove disconsolately back to Milford.

There had been no word from Reverend Lawson but Belinda expected him back from Winchester by the weekend. Perhaps his friend, Sir Gerald, had been able to shed some light on the tapestry. That at least was something to look forward to.

That and dinner and the theatre with Mark on Saturday night.

Reverend Lawson eagerly let himself into the Vicarage. His time spent with Sir Gerald had been more productive than he could have imagined. Apart from his pilgrimage to Jane Austen's grave, the exciting news regarding the tapestry had made the journey to Winchester more than worthwhile. It was with some reluctance that he departed for Milford but there was his Sunday service to attend to and as he turned the key in the Vicarage door on the Saturday night his first thought was to telephone Belinda and convey his thrilling news.

He knew that Mrs Darby would have prepared the altar and Miss Hilgood would have selected the hymns that she would proceed to torture on the organ the following morning.

He skimmed quickly through the letters his housekeeper, Miss Davidson, had left in a neat pile on the hallstand before making his way through the chill cottage to the telephone.

His fingers, warm from the thick gloves he had worn on his return journey, came in contact with the cold dial of the telephone and he shivered and reminded himself to turn on the heating before he retired. He doubted if he would be able to sleep until he had told Belinda of what he had learnt in Winchester.

The telephone rang in Belinda's darkened house. Three times it rang before there was a mechanical click and Belinda's metallic recorded voice advised the Vicar she was unable to take the call and please leave a message and she would return the call as soon as possible.

'Damn!' Reverend Lawson permitted himself the strongest expletive in his vocabulary.

The telephone beeped and immediately he began to stutter, his usual reaction when forced to leave a message on the infernal new invention. He felt foolish talking to an appliance.

'Er ... Miss Lawrence? That is ... Belinda? I'm back from Winchester ... er ... that is ... I mean ... I think we should talk as soon as possible. Sir Gerald was a wonderful help ... and there is the most exciting news about your tapestry. Will you ring me? Er ... What do I do now? ... Er ... that is all.'

Wondering if he should have concluded "over and out," he replaced the receiver. His nerves, he knew, would not permit him a restful sleep until he had spoken to Belinda, so to calm himself he reached for the decanter and poured himself an unusually stiff brandy. The wonderful liquid coursed its way down, spreading its natural warmth and comfort. He sighed with satisfaction but automatically began to pace back and forth across the small room. A sudden thought occurred to him and he reached for the telephone again. As he dialled Belinda's number he smiled at her concern in letting the tapestry out of her possession.

'I must let her know that it is in safe hands,' he chuckled, as he listened again to Belinda's recorded voice. When the beeps ceased he left his message. He took another sip of his brandy.

The clock ticked off five minutes, its loud tick-tock the only sound in the silent house.

'Oh, come on woman,' he muttered anxiously, willing Belinda to answer his call. The news he had to impart was burning his lips and he glanced anxiously at his watch. It was just before midnight.

As if in answer to his prayers he heard the squeak of his garden gate and the sound of footsteps on the path. 'Thank God. It's her,' murmured the Vicar, as he put down his near empty glass. Fumbling with the light switch he rushed into the hall. It was only as he was opening the door to admit Belinda that he realised only a few minutes had passed since he left the message on the machine; she would not have had time to have heard it, let alone drive the distance from her house to the Vicarage.

As the grandfather clock in the hall struck midnight, Belinda pressed the play button on the answering machine. The recording device was faulty and the tape stretched, so that the Reverend's voice distorted and moaned slowly as the worn tape first wowed ponderously, then sped up to a comical screech. It was not aided by a rather exhilarated and confused Reverend Lawson. Belinda played it back twice to confirm his message of exciting news, before the exhausted tape whimpered to a halt.

She rummaged in a drawer for a new cassette she'd recently bought and replaced the worn tape. She dropped the old cassette into the waste paper basket and switched off the light. 'It's far too late to call back,' she sighed 'he's probably dead to the world by now.'

Climbing the stairs to her bedroom, Belinda decided that she would attend the morning Communion service and have coffee with the Vicar after the ceremony during which he could tell her his good news. As she switched off the electric blanket and slipped between the warm sheets she wondered what the Vicar could possibly have learnt about the tapestry that he found so exciting. She also realised, guiltily, she had not attended church for some months and her intended visit was not driven by religious motives but rather by curiosity. With these self-reproachful thoughts she slipped into a deep and satisfying sleep.

The dank air of the church chilled Belinda as she stepped into the gloomy interior. No more than half a dozen parishioners sat scattered about the pews, each in their familiar positions, which they guarded with ferocity should anyone stumble into their territory. They each sat as far away from their neighbour as they could get.

Belinda walked up the aisle and took a vacant seat three rows back from the altar. Her arrival was greeted by unfriendly stares from the congregation.

Mrs Darby and the Misses Hilgood and Davidson stood near the organ, each vibrating with tension.

Like the three witches from Macbeth, thought Belinda.

The sorcerers gave a disparaging glance to Belinda, a suspicious glare as though suspecting an infiltrator. Even though Belinda had been living in the village now for two years she was still considered an outsider and she suspected that eighty years from now the position would be much the same. She glanced at her watch. The vicar was late. It was already ten minutes past the regular starting time for the service.

The three witches whispered amongst themselves.

Mrs Darby looked cross.

Miss Hilgood kept glancing at her watch and towards the door.

Miss Davidson was wringing her hands.

Someone coughed uncomfortably and Belinda looked back at the meagre congregation. Blank stares and vacant expressions met her enquiring look.

A further five minutes past and there was a restless atmosphere building up within the church.

Belinda rose and walked towards the three women. They eyed her much as they would have inspected the Whore of Babylon.

'Excuse me, is anything wrong?' Belinda asked.

The three furies exchanged glances. Mrs Darby was first to chance talking to the newcomer. 'It's the Vicar,' she snapped belligerently. 'He's been away. On a holiday.' She spat out the word as though it was an obscenity and conveyed the impression that, in her view a clergyman was not entitled to such a luxury.

'Yes, I know,' replied Belinda.

Six eyes widened in curiosity as to why Belinda should be party to this information.

'But he came back last night.' Six eyes popped as this up-to-date news was absorbed. 'He left a message for me last night. He said he wanted to see me.'

Exchanged glances silently transmitted the common thought that this was a scoop and details would have to be gleaned, expertly and as soon as possible.

Mrs Darby wiggled her shoulders in affronted irritation. 'I spent all yesterday afternoon polishing the candlesticks and doing the flowers,' she pouted, 'and the least the Vicar could do is to make sure he is on time for the service.'

'Have you checked at the Vicarage?' asked Belinda, looking from one woman to the other. 'He may have slept in. Or he may be ill.'

This disagreeable suggestion made the three women uncomfortable.

Miss Hilgood looked down her long thin nose, disdaining any reply.

Miss Davidson primly adjusted her hat. 'I tried knocking but there was no answer. And I tried the key but the door is locked from inside. I'm his housekeeper,' she concluded virtuously, seeing Belinda's curiosity.

'Well, I know he's back from Winchester,' Belinda said, turning and walking back down the aisle, 'so something must be wrong.'

The entire congregation, sensing something more exciting than the Communion service, fell in line behind her and followed her next door to the Vicarage.

The key, as Miss Davidson had predicted, would not open the lock and there was no reply to repeated knocking. The housekeeper preened herself in righteous affirmation of her testimony.

'There's only one thing for it,' said Belinda, 'we'll have to break in.'

A kitchen window proved to be unlocked, and with the help of a rubbish bin, which made a shaky ladder, and the steadying hands of the parishioners, Belinda, being the youngest and therefore the most agile, was able to climb through and into the kitchen.

'Reverend Lawson?' But the silence in the house was almost tangible. Stepping with caution she walked into the hall and made her way into the unfamiliar cottage. On her left was a small room that appeared to be the Vicar's study. His desk drawers were upturned and papers littered the floor.

Belinda felt tense with apprehension as she approached the front drawing room and pushed open the door.

The room was in confusion and in the centre of it, on the floor, lay the Vicar.

Belinda's legs went weak and she clutched at the doorframe for support.

The Vicar had been mutilated. One eye had been gouged out and his right thigh slashed open to reveal the bone.

Four

Hazel Whitby kicked off her shoes, wriggled her toes ecstatically in front of the roaring fire, and willingly accepted her first gin and tonic of the day.

'Would someone tell me why I'm stupid enough to attend funerals?' She took a reassuring gulp. 'Depressing events, unfashionable clothes, snivelling mourners, muddy shoes, not to mention the possibility of catching pneumonia.'

'It was the least we could do,' answered Belinda, pulling off her black coat. She warmed her hands in front of the fire. Mark handed her a glass of sherry.

'I don't see why. It isn't as though he was family or even if we were regular churchgoers.'

'He was a nice old man,' said Belinda defensively.

'Granted, but I see no reason for us to attend his funeral.' Mark stretched full length on the sofa. Belinda placed her glass on the mantelpiece and looked at her two companions.

'Talk about the "me" generation. The Vicar was murdered. Killed in the most horrible way. Surely he deserved our sympathy and the only way we could show it was to attend his funeral. Besides …'

'Besides what?' asked Hazel, waving an already empty glass at Mark. He ignored her.

'Well, it gave us a chance to check out the mourners.'

Mark was incredulous. 'You didn't really expect that the murderer would turn up at the funeral?'

'Well, why not? Surely you've heard of the criminal returning to the scene of the crime?'

'That's "dogs to their vomit",' replied Mark in a superior tone.

Hazel sighed. 'Really, Belinda. Did you *see* who attended the funeral? The average age would've been two hundred and fifty at the most conservative. Do you really think any one of them would have had the strength to lift a weapon against the Vicar? They were so old I wonder at the wisdom of their leaving the graveyard.'

Mark snorted in amusement while Belinda frowned at the two of them.

'The point is, were there any strangers there? Strangers to the village?'

'Of course there were.' Mark rose to refresh Hazel's glass. 'But they were all old associates of the Vicar, mainly religious colleagues. Hardly the sort given to violent murder.'

'And what you're forgetting,' added Hazel dryly, '*if* you accept that one of the old fuddy-duddies killed Reverend Lawson, then you *must* suspect them of killing Mr William de Whatever.'

'De Montfort,' corrected Belinda thoughtfully. What Hazel said was valid. Both men had died in the same manner. Eyes gouged out and their thighs slashed open.

'So what's the connection?' Belinda looked from one to the other.

Mark shrugged noncommittally. Hazel was reticent. She shook her glass making the ice cube rattle.

'You must agree there has to be some connection?'

But her companions were silent. Belinda gave an exasperated sigh. 'All right. Let's start with the funeral. OK, so the mourners were old friends, or so it appears. But there were villagers there. Let's examine them. Firstly, Mrs Darby ...'

Mark laughed. 'You don't really think that old biddy did the Vicar in? Next you'll be telling us that you suspect a plot between the Misses Hilgood and Davidson to bump off the Vicar, take over the parish and become the high priests of a world-dominating feminist sect.'

'And if it was one of them,' continued Hazel caustically, 'can you see them zooming up to York to do in your Mr de Mountebank?'

'No. I don't think they killed him. But someone did. And in the same way they killed the Vicar.'

'You're stating the obvious,' yawned Mark.

Belinda shook her fists in frustration. 'Obvious yes, but why? Why were two men killed and in the same bizarre way? What was the common thread?'

Hazel put her empty glass down deliberately on the table. She eyed both her young companions. 'The tapestry.'

Belinda and Mark looked at her. 'Are you serious?' Mark asked cynically.

'Of course she is,' cried Belinda. She felt relief that someone else felt as she did.

'I know it sounds absurd, but I suspect that bloody piece of tat is trouble. I felt it from the start, even though I couldn't and still can't say why. But there it is. Two men are dead and I believe the tapestry is the cause.' Hazel folded her arms, defying the others to challenge her statement.

Mark shook his head in disbelief and turned to Belinda. 'Where's the tapestry?'

'At the Vicarage. Reverend Lawson took it to Winchester for his friend to inspect. He rang me when he returned. I was going to collect it on the Sunday morning, but after he was killed the police sealed the Vicarage and no one was allowed in, so I imagine it's still there. I'll get it as soon as the police will let me in.'

But it wasn't at the Vicarage.

Inspector Jordan, who was investigating the murder, was helpful by permitting Belinda to inspect the late Vicar's overnight bag that had accompanied him on his journey.

'And you say the purpose of his visit to this Sir Gerald, was to investigate the origins of a missing piece of tapestry?' Inspector Jordan popped a cough lozenge into his mouth. He was susceptible to colds and flu.

As the person who had discovered the corpse, Belinda had been interrogated thoroughly by the Inspector and she had explained the Vicar's offer of identifying the tapestry. 'Yes. It seems his friend in Winchester had experience with things like that.'

They were standing in the Vicarage room where the murder had occurred. Belinda glanced down to where the crimson stain still saturated the carpet. A violent image of the raw flesh and sightless eye socket of the murdered man leapt into her imagination. Feeling weak, she turned her attention back to the open overnight bag.

'I'm sure he would have brought the tapestry back with him. He knew how anxious I was about letting it out of my hands. He had something to tell me.'

'Was it that valuable?' Inspector Jordan cleared a tickle in his throat.

'I don't know if it was of any value at all,' replied Belinda, but even as she said it, Hazel's words rang in her ear.

'Well, we've searched the cottage but found nothing like the tapestry you describe. If you say it was of no value then it couldn't have been the motive for the murder.'

'You don't believe the tapestry was the reason he was killed?'

'I just said that I didn't. That is, if there is no monetary value attached to the tapestry.' The Inspector paused, surreptitiously wiping his nose with his finger. 'However, there is always the possibility that it had another sort of value for someone else.'

'Was anything stolen?' Belinda asked.

'His wallet and some church money he was holding. Probably someone looking for money for drugs. Not worth a human life, but it's common enough these days.'

Belinda nodded an agreement she did not feel. If the tapestry was not in the Vicarage it must have been stolen. Unless … unless it was still in Winchester.

'Didn't the Inspector comment on the similarity with the murder in York?'

Mark and Belinda were walking down Gay Street. Mark had been inspecting a house in The Circus whose owner was considering selling. Belinda accompanied him, having heard the house, now the talk of Bath, had been redecorated in spectacular style.

'He muttered something about talking to the Yorkshire police, so I imagine they are comparing notes.'

'You didn't tell him that you were in York just before the murder?'

'I don't want to get involved in a second murder. Besides, what happened in York was well after we'd left Kidbrooke House.'

'But you believe the killings are connected.'

'Yes. But how to prove it?'

They walked on in silence for a few moments. Belinda was wrestling with a crazy idea. 'Mark. What would you say if I told you I was thinking of joining the Holy Rollers?'

Mark's expression hardly changed. 'I'd say you'd finally gone daft.'

'Maybe, but I'm convinced that the Godwins are tied up in this somehow. The only way I can think of getting to know them and observe them is to join in their activities.'

'By becoming a nun?' Mark gave an irreverent smile.

'If that's what it takes. But seriously, Mark, look at the facts. They knew about Kidbrooke House. Came looking for furniture Hazel bought in the auction and their name is the same as that of King Harold.'

Mark stopped in his tracks. 'What? '

'It's true. Reverend Lawson told me that King Harold's family name was Godwin, and the Godwins run the Fellowship of St Augustine.'

Mark walked on. 'As I said. Daft.'

Belinda hurried after him. 'I know it sounds crazy, but I'm convinced they're involved somehow and it all has something to do with the missing tapestry.'

Mark shook his head in disbelief. 'Well, you're on your own. I'll have nothing to do with it.'

'Yes, you will. I want you to track down the Vicar's friend in Winchester.'

'Why?'

'Because he told the Vicar something about the tapestry, something that excited him. And I want to know what it was. Besides, it's possible that the tapestry is still in Winchester. I only assumed that the Vicar brought it back with him.'

'But if that's the case, why was the Vicar killed? You believe the tapestry was the reason he was murdered.'

Belinda thrust her fists deep into her coat pocket. Mark was right. Was it possible it was just a drug-related murder?

'What's his name, this friend in Winchester?'

'All I know is his name is Sir Gerald.'

'That's it? Sir Gerald?'

'Afraid so.'

'You're a great help.'

'The Vicar did mention his full name in passing but I can't remember it. So it's Sir Gerald in Winchester.'

Mark shrugged in disbelief. 'Well … I'll ask my father. He may be able to help through the old-boy network. But don't hold out any hopes.'

Belinda gave him a grateful smile. 'I knew I could count on you. Now I'm off to Norton St Philip to take the veil.'

As she parked her car under the Fellowship of St Augustine sign and walked down the slope towards the farmhouse, Belinda suddenly had second thoughts. Could she convince the Godwins that she seriously wanted to pursue a religious life? And what did that entail? After all, she had no idea of the principles they conformed to. Did they follow general Christian beliefs?

Lost in her thoughts, she did not see a young woman approach her.

'May the grace of God be with you.'

Belinda gave a start and turned to face the girl.

'My name is Marianne. Do you wish to see the Master?'

Belinda took in the girl's appearance. She appeared no older than sixteen, with dark hair and bright dark eyes. She wore a thick woollen pullover and men's trousers, which were tucked into Wellington boots. She smiled a rather melancholy smile. Belinda wondered if she was a trifle simple.

'The Master?'

The girl nodded and began to walk towards the front door of the house. 'I expect you do,' she said, 'there really isn't any point talking to anyone else, except of course the Mistress.'

'Do you mean Mr and Mrs Godwin?' Belinda hurried to catch up to the girl. The girl did not reply but stopped at the front door.

'There is a bell inside the hall. If you ring it, someone will see to you. Now I must go and prepare for the Angelus.' She turned on her heel and hurried around to the back of the building. The deep clanging of a bell rang through the air, to be followed by voices singing a hymn. Belinda lifted the latch on the door and entered the hall of the farmhouse.

Incense perfumed the air, along with the penetrating smell of candles that had burnt down and extinguished themselves. Several closed doors faced into the hall. The singing increased in volume as Belinda made her way into the wood panelled vestibule. She picked up a small brass bell and rang it. The sharp tinkle cut through the chanting voices.

Belinda glanced around the walls. They were bare apart from a framed picture of a mediaeval saint whom she took to be St Augustine. There was no reply to her summons and she was reaching for the bell a second time, when the door at the far end of the hall opened and a figure in grey monk's robes emerged. The chanting had increased as he opened the door and subsided as the monk closed it. Belinda concluded that the Angeles ceremony was being celebrated in that room. The monk folded his arms into his sleeves and approached slowly, his leather sandals slapping gently against the bare wooden floor.

He was no older than eighteen or so and Belinda recognised him as the second monk she had seen arguing with William de Montfort. He was also the man that she and Mark had almost run down in a lane-way the day they drove to the farm. His manner then had been very hostile.

'May the grace of God be with you.' His voice revealed a London accent and Belinda imagined that if he had been dressed in jeans and T-shirt he would be indistinguishable from any youth in South Kensington.

'I'd like to talk to Mr Godwin.'

The youthful monk ran his eyes over Belinda in what she thought was a distinctly unreligious manner. Nevertheless when he replied it was in a whisper. 'The Master is at prayer at the moment.' He turned to one of the nearby doors. 'If you wait in here, the Master will be with you at the end of the service.'

He flung open the door and gestured for Belinda to enter. As she brushed past him, Belinda detected the faint smell of marijuana. *So, smoking pot is permitted. I wonder what other pleasures are practised?* she thought as she entered the small room. The door swung shut behind her and she heard the slap-slap of the monk's sandals as he returned to prayer.

Two uncomfortable looking chairs, a small desk and a bookcase were the only furnishings. Belinda inspected the books. They appeared to be mostly liturgical works and religious tracts.

She sank down on the least uncomfortable looking chair and waited. Chanting and bells continued faintly and Belinda began to wonder if she had made a mistake. Maybe the Godwins were just a couple of religious eccentrics and had no interest in the tapestry.

But the evidence of her own eyes witnessing the monks at Kidbrooke House quickly drove any doubt from her mind.

Lost in her thoughts, Belinda was startled when the door was suddenly flung open and Mr Godwin appeared. He stood, rather dramatically, Belinda thought, framed in the doorway. For a moment his eyes revealed his surprise at seeing Belinda, but he quickly recovered and stepped into the room closing the door firmly behind him.

'This is a surprise. A pleasant surprise, Miss Lawrence. I must confess that I hardly expected you to visit our little community. May I ask what brings you here?' He had not taken his gaze from Belinda and continued to keep his eyes on her as he took a seat opposite.

He's baffled, but glad I'm here, thought Belinda.

Aloud she said, 'I heard you have a religious group here. Lately I've been questioning my faith. My attitudes towards life. The material world bothers me and I am searching for some spiritual support.'

Belinda wondered if she sounded convincing? She thought it sounded a little too pat, however Godwin seemed to accept her at face value. He nodded the nod of a sage.

'The world is indeed concerned with material wealth at the expense of spiritual values.' He frowned and looked keenly at Belinda. 'But surely you practise your faith? You are Anglican?' He raised an interrogating eyebrow.

Belinda nodded. 'I am looking for more. Besides, my local Vicar died recently … under rather horrible circumstances.' She watched Godwin's face for a sign of acknowledgement but was disappointed. His face was a mask.

'Yes,' he replied, examining a fingernail, 'I heard that he'd died. Tragic. The world is full of sinful actions.' He settled back into his chair. 'So you are looking for more? What do you know of our community?'

'Nothing really.' Belinda wondered if the man was totally convinced of her search for faith.

'We here at the fellowship are dedicated to the ideals of the great St Augustine. Do you know of St Augustine?'

Belinda shook her head. 'I've heard of him, but I was educated in Australia. I'm really only now discovering English history.'

Godwin was silent for a moment, then rose and walked to the window. He addressed Belinda with his back to her. 'Augustine was sent from Rome in 597 along with a party of forty monks. His holy task was to convert the barbaric English to Christianity. To the monks' surprise they were welcomed here and Augustine converted King Ethelbert. It's said that he baptised over ten thousand converts on Christmas Day.'

'Here in Bath?'

Godwin turned to face her, a superior smile on his lips. 'No. Canterbury. The king gave Augustine his own palace in Canterbury and later Augustine founded an Abbey just outside the walls of the city. The ruins are still there.'

'Did he build Canterbury Cathedral as well?'

Again the superior smile. 'No, but the present cathedral is built on the site of Augustine's original church.'

He took his place opposite Belinda and looked hard into her eyes. Distrustful as she was, Belinda felt his magnetism and charm.

'We try to follow the simple life of Augustine and early Christians by meditation, prayer and human interaction, with as little influence from the outside world as possible. As you can see, we have a farm and we're pretty much self-supporting. Our daily routine involves prayer and contemplation intermingled with work. Much as the early monks did.'

'I see,' said Belinda, in what she thought was a suitably

subservient voice, 'but can anyone join? I mean, could I?'

'We take people on trust to begin with. There is a period of initiation; a noviciate, if you will. After a time, one can become either a full member or, as we call them, an associate. That is one who does not live in but practises our beliefs nonetheless. The full members are baptised and are permitted to wear the robes of St Augustine. The associates may live outside the community but come here to pray and enter into our activities.'

'That sounds as though it would suit me,' said Belinda.

'You don't feel you're ready to leave the world?'

Not on your life, said Belinda to herself. To Godwin she presented an apologetic gesture. 'I believe it would take time for me to adjust.'

Godwin nodded thoughtfully. 'You're probably correct. After all, many are called but few are chosen.' He rose and moved to the door. 'As I explain our beliefs to you, I'll show you around our chapel.'

Belinda followed him into the hall and they walked to the far door. Godwin opened it and ushered Belinda in. She found herself in a large room with windows along one side. It would have been the central communal room in the original farmhouse but was now converted into something resembling a chapel. At the far end was a wooden table, draped by a white cloth. On it, a large cottage loaf of home-made bread and a glass pitcher of water. There were about twenty chairs spread about the room, all facing the altar. Above, on the wall, was a plain wooden cross.

As they stepped into the room, Godwin offered Belinda a small brass bowl. She recoiled from it in horror.

It was filled with blood!

A smile crossed Godwin's face. 'It is only coloured water. We use it as a reminder of the blood spilled by the Saviour.' He dipped a finger into the ruby coloured water and touched the fluid to his lips. 'This is our chapel, the focus point of our community. We have morning, midday and evening prayers here. The community is encouraged to pray or meditate here whenever they feel the need.'

He turned away to replace the brass bowl and Belinda looked about her. Along the walls, on either side leading up to the altar, was a series of framed paintings. On closer inspection she realised that they were not paintings but a succession of colour photographs. With a shock Belinda recognised them as illustrations of the Bayeux Tapestry.

But they were incomplete.

They began and ended with the Battle of Hastings and the assassination of King Harold.

Five

Chimes from the bells of Bath Abbey penetrated into the bedroom. Belinda and Mark sprawled in Mark's huge bed, the picture of Sunday morning indolence.

They had spent the previous Saturday night at the cinema where the latest feel-good film had been screening. The plot would not have tested the intelligence of a four-year-old and Belinda and Mark had left the cinema early, dined on a speedy meal of pasta and had fallen into bed before the ten o'clock news had spread its mantle of despondency.

Now, brioche crumbs littered the bed-sheets and coffee dregs cooled as Mark perused the Sunday papers. Belinda idly flicked through a colour supplement. Mark yawned widely and waved the paper at Belinda.

'There's a follow-up story to the Vicar's murder.'

Belinda grasped the page. 'Police believe there is no connection between the murder of Mr William de Montfort in Yorkshire and the more recent murder of the Reverend Lawson in Somerset even though the manner in which they met their death was similar.' She crushed the paper in disgust. 'How can they say that? Their deaths were identical.'

'Perhaps they just said that to put the murderer off guard.'

Belinda shook her shoulders in annoyance. 'But there has to be a connection.'

'So you keep saying,' yawned Mark slipping lower into the bed. 'Are you still going ahead with your plan to find God?'

Belinda prodded him irritably. 'Don't blaspheme. As a matter of fact I'm due at the commune this afternoon for my induction as an associate of the Fellowship.'

'How sexy,' murmured Mark. 'Will you wear a veil and have your hair cut off, like Audrey Hepburn?'

Belinda giggled in spite of herself. 'Don't be daft. No. It's just an introduction. I expect Godwin will elaborate on what he's already told me. Show me the ropes, that sort of thing.'

'Ropes?' cried Mark with amused interest. 'Is he into bondage? I didn't know you fancied a bit of S & M. It sheds a rather attractive light on your character.'

'Idiot,' Belinda laughed, as she hit him with the rolled up newspaper.

'Oh, yes please. More. More,' pleaded Mark with fake pleasure.

Belinda giggled and snuggled up against Mark's warm body, knocking a coffee cup and saucer onto the floor in the process.

'Careful,' cried Mark in mock distress. 'That's the last of the family heirlooms.'

'Talking of family,' murmured Belinda into his ear, 'has your father tracked down Sir Gerald's address in Winchester?' She gently bit his earlobe.

'While you're being beaten black and blue by Godwin this afternoon, I'll be visiting the oldies. Should have something to report tonight.'

Belinda ran her hand up his thigh and for the next forty minutes or so neither gave any thought to tapestries, religion or murder.

'Sexual licence is the curse of our present society,' said Charles Godwin in a sanctimonious voice.

Belinda nodded a silent endorsement she did not wholly subscribe to. Inwardly she smiled at Godwin's chosen terminology and wondered where exactly one purchased a sexual licence.

Godwin had led her down to the banks of the stream and Belinda was glad he had offered her a pair of Wellington boots. The soil was muddy and slippery.

She had spent some time at her wardrobe choosing the right sort of garb for her interview with Godwin. After trying on several outfits she had settled on a rather prim cotton print dress that was several years old and distinctly homely. How it had ever ended up in her wardrobe she couldn't imagine. It was far too cold to be wearing just a cotton dress, so she had hauled on a heavy sheepskin coat that she had brought with her from Australia.

As an additional aid in her pursuit of religious piety, Belinda had removed all her makeup, had thrown a scarf over her hair, and tied it under her chin. Looking in the mirror she was reminded of newsreel images she had seen of refugees fleeing from advancing armies and was thankful, not for the first time in her life, for cosmetics and fashionable ready-to-wear.

She wondered if she should have been carrying a devout tome such as the Book of Common Prayer, but decided that her plain dress was sufficient evidence of her convictions and any enhancement would be gilding the lily.

'In dealing with the young, we find that temptations of the flesh are the hardest struggles they have to overcome,' continued Godwin, as they made their way back from the stream towards the farmhouse.

'Do you have many young members?' Belinda sidestepped a cowpat.

'Only a handful actually sanctioned as full members.'

'You mean monks?'

Godwin smiled. 'If you mean the ones who wear monks' robes, yes. It's their own choice to wear the robes and then only here, as they move around the community.'

'But sometimes they've been seen in Norton St Philip.'

Godwin glanced at her. 'Occasionally some of the more excitable members forget themselves and do wear their robes in the streets. They see it as a sign of their faith and are proud to display it.'

And parade it as far away as York, thought Belinda.

They approached a large barn at the rear of the house and, as if in answer to Belinda's thoughts, a young monk and a girl emerged. The man had his arm around the girl's waist and they were both sniggering lewdly over some amusing joke.

Belinda drew in a sharp breath. It was the aggressive monk from York. She sensed Godwin stiffen as he saw the couple. In turn, the giggling twosome froze as they came face to face with Godwin. The man dropped his hand from the girl's hips. For a moment the two men looked at each other, the older stern and rigid, the younger insolently fingering the small silver cross that hung from the earring in his pierced ear.

Then the young man, with a brazen smirk, nudged the girl and the two set off towards the house. The girl glanced back at them and gave a crude giggle.

Godwin watched them go. Belinda was surprised at the expression of hostility on his face. Aware that Belinda was watching him, he turned to her and gave a shrug of his shoulders. 'As I said, urges of the flesh are the hardest trials for the young.'

'Who is he?'

'We know him as Brother Saul,' replied Godwin through tight lips. He turned and began to walk quickly towards the house, so that Belinda struggled to keep up with him. 'It is our belief that an hour's meditation a day is an ideal way to begin,' Godwin said loudly over his shoulder, 'so I suggest you spend some time in the chapel, now that you are here.'

They deposited their muddy boots at the door and proceeded into the dark interior of the house. Godwin led the way through a kitchen and dinning area and into the main hall. He opened the door to the chapel and ushered Belinda in. Taking up a large Bible, he flipped through pages and opened them at a chosen passage.

'For today, I suggest you contemplate the Second Book of Kings, Chapter Five, verses one to five. It'd be wise for you to come here each day for a week, spend an hour in chapel, and at the end of that time we can review your vocation.' He thrust the Bible into Belinda's hands and, with a curt nod, hurried from the room.

Belinda sank down onto a hard wooden chair and gazed around her. The chapel looked the same as her first visit, except – except something was missing. Belinda stood and walked towards the table used as the altar. The cottage loaf was still there, but now a green mould was beginning to grow on the side of the bread. The pitcher of water had a thin layer of dust over the surface. Then Belinda realised what was missing.

The colour photographs of the Bayeux Tapestry had been taken down.

A sudden movement beside her made Belinda jump and she turned in fright.

'May the grace of God be with you.'

Beside her was the girl she had met on her first visit. Mabel? Maureen? No, Marianne. The girl gave a silent smile. Again Belinda wondered if she was simpleminded.

'You frightened me,' said Belinda. 'I didn't hear you come in. I was just looking for the photographs of the Bayeux Tapestry. They were here when I first came, but now they've gone.'

The girl nodded but gave no reply.

This is going to be a hard slog, thought Belinda grimly. She asked, 'Why have they taken the photographs away?'

Marianne looked at her as though she doubted that anyone did not know the answer. 'Because the time for mourning has passed.'

'Mourning? What mourning?'

'The six weeks of mourning, of course.'

'Mourning for whom?'

Marianne looked at her in amazement. 'Why, for King Harold, of course. For the anniversary of his death on the twenty-sixth of October –'

'*Marianne.*'

A deep authoritarian voice rang out through the chapel. At the door stood Mrs Godwin, a grim expression on her face. Belinda felt Marianne flinch.

'Marianne, you must leave Miss Lawrence in peace. You know the rules about talking during meditation.'

Belinda stepped forward. 'I'm afraid it was my fault. I spoke to her. I'm not familiar with the rules yet.'

Mrs Godwin ran her eyes over Belinda. 'My husband advised me that you were to be with us for a time.' Her eyes flicked back to the cowering Marianne. 'Nevertheless, Marianne knows better.' She held her hand out to the girl. 'You will come along with me now, Marianne. Leave Miss Lawrence to meditate.'

Without looking at Belinda, Marianne shuffled out of the room. With a glance and a nod, Mrs Godwin closed the chapel door. Belinda was alone in the silent room. She sank down on a chair, glanced at the Bible and read the first line of the passage selected by Godwin.

"Behold we are thy bone and thy flesh."

Belinda distractedly closed the book. Why would the community be mourning the death of a king who died nearly a thousand years ago? And what of Saul, the so-called monk? And his girl friend?

Was it just coincidence that the Godwins knew about the auction at Kidbrooke House? And who broke into Hazel's shop to carve the inscription on the table?

The Godwins?

It was beginning to look like it. The Latin inscription read, "King Harold was killed", while here in their chapel they held a mourning period for the dead king.

If that was so, were they searching for the tapestry?

But what was the value of the tapestry to them?

The tapestry celebrated the coronation of William the Conqueror. The man who defeated King Harold.

The Vicar's message said he had exciting news about the tapestry and Sir Gerald had been a wonderful help. She hoped that Mark's father had been able to track down the mysterious Sir Gerald.

Belinda glanced at her watch realising that her time of meditation was over and she was no nearer to solving any part of the puzzle. She rose and turned to go. As she did, the door opened and a figure in monk's robes entered. Belinda recognised the young monk who had attended to her on her first visit. He ignored her and, folding his hands into the sleeves of his robe, sank down in an attitude of silent prayer. Belinda tiptoed towards the door.

In a corner at the rear of the room, high up on the wall, was a small balcony with a wooden railing. As she glanced up at the balcony, the door leading to it swung shut. Belinda shivered as though someone had walked over her grave.

Had someone been watching her from the balcony?

She stepped out into the entrance hall. It was silent and dark. No other member of the community seemed to be in the building. Belinda looked to her left and saw that leading off the hall was a small shadowy passageway. With a glance around her, she stepped softly across the hall and entered the passage. It ran down along the rear wall of the chapel and led to a heavy wooden door.

Belinda turned the handle. The door swung open. She stepped into what appeared to be a small storage room. There were a few chairs stacked against the wall and a pile of Bibles. Leaning against the wall was a number of picture frames with their backs to her. Belinda pulled one away from the wall. It was one of the colour photographs of the Bayeux Tapestry.

Behind her was a steep narrow staircase that led up to a door high in the wall. Belinda replaced the photograph and mounted the stairs. Reaching the door, she opened it and found herself on the balcony looking down into the chapel. She leant over the railing and saw that the monk was still below. Any pretensions towards prayer had been discarded. The man had his feet stretched out on the seat in front and was dragging heavily on a cigarette. His interest was given over to a paperback novel that claimed his full attention. The biting smoke from his cigarette floated upwards and Belinda gagged as she involuntarily inhaled the fumes.

Covering her nose with her hand, Belinda silently stepped back onto the stairs and began to descend. She had just reached the bottom step, when the door opened and Mrs Godwin entered.

'What are you doing in here?' she demanded in a hoarse aggressive voice.

'I'm afraid I lost my way,' said Belinda, 'I couldn't find the front door.'

Mrs Godwin stared at her unbelievingly. She put down an armful of books and taking Belinda roughly by the arm, led her into the entrance hall. She pointed at the front door.

'You'll find that's the way out.'

Belinda thanked her meekly and headed towards the exit. As she closed the door she looked back. Mrs Godwin was watching her with a rigid look of suspicion. All the way up the driveway to her car she could feel the woman's eyes following her. It was with a sigh of relief that she heard the engine start and felt the car move forward to take her home.

As she drove towards Milford, the words from the Bible returned to disturb her.

"Behold, we are thy bone and thy flesh."

The washing machine whirred into life as Belinda shut the laundry door behind her. Sunday evening was her washing day and with the luxury of an automatic machine and a dryer, her week's washing was no longer a chore.

There had been no message from Mark when she returned from the commune, only a slurred mumble on the message machine from Hazel, indicating that she had overdone her daily consumption of gin. She asked Belinda to take care of the shop the next day, as she was going to inspect some antique silver for sale in Itchen Abbas, a village in Hampshire.

'Some old duck snuffed it and the family don't know the value of her belongings – I hope,' Hazel's voice slurred from the machine.

Belinda poured herself a coffee and, taking her aunt's cumbersome King James Bible from the shelf, sank onto the sofa. She opened the page at the Second Book of Kings, Chapter Five, verses one to five.

"Behold, we are thy bone and thy flesh."

Search as she might, Belinda could not find any particular point that she could be expected to meditate upon. The passage dealt with the anointing of David as king over Israel and while she found it interesting historically she thought the passage irrelevant and not the least spiritual.

'Why would Godwin expect me to find anything uplifting in that passage?'

The telephone rang as she put aside the heavy Bible.

'Shall I come over and lick your wounds?' said Mark in a mock lascivious voice.

Belinda smiled. 'If you are referring to your S & M fantasies of this morning, forget it. Godwin was a model of decorum. The only pain I had was trying to find meaning in an obscure passage from the Bible.'

'Ah.' Mark sounded disappointed. 'Well, I have some good news for you. The old man has been able to track down the elusive Sir Gerald.'

'Well done,' cried Belinda, reaching for a pencil and note pad. 'Let's have the details.'

'His name is Sir Gerald Taylor. I'm pretty certain he's our man. Fairly crusty old academic, it seems. Expert in mediaeval history and all that.' He gave Belinda the address and telephone number for Sir Gerald in Winchester. Belinda jotted them down.

'Thanks, Mark. Now get off the line. I want to ring Sir Gerald immediately.'

'Is that all the thanks I get? Get off the line? I ask you? Where's your sense of appreciation?'

'You'll get thanked next weekend. Now, go.'

'I'll hold you to that promise,' said Mark, as he hung up.

Belinda looked at the address. 'Let's hope Sir Gerald is willing to help.' She dialled the Winchester number and waited as the ringing tone at the other end rang and rang. Belinda gave an exasperated sigh. 'Please. Please. Be there!'

But the ringing tone was her only answer. In despair, she was just about to hang up, when there was a click and a bright melodious voice said, '4695.'

'Oh, Sir Gerald,' she began to gabble, as she introduced herself. Somehow in her confusion she managed to explain she owned the tapestry that the Vicar had shown him and wished to meet with him, tomorrow if possible.

'Well, let me see,' replied the academic, 'that should be possible. I was planning a trip to Sussex, but that can wait until later in the week. I suggest eleven o'clock, if that's agreeable with you.'

Belinda would have agreed to meeting at six a.m. if it meant talking to the man. She readily agreed, after assuring him that she had his address.

As she hung up the telephone and searched for the road directory, she realised that she had forgotten to ask if he still had the tapestry in his possession.

'I'll know soon enough,' she told herself by way of taking comfort and reached for the road map. As she traced the route that she would take to Winchester, her eye fell upon a familiar name.

Itchen Abbas.

'That's the village Hazel's going to. We can travel down together.' She dialled Hazel's phone number, but the reply was a steady ring-ring. Belinda realised that her friend was more than likely in a gin-induced sleep. She would have to talk to her first thing in the morning.

Reaching for her mobile phone, she stored Sir Gerald's number in the memory dialling facility and allocated a recall number. As she dropped the phone into her shoulder bag and climbed the stairs to her bedroom, Belinda's mind was in a whirl of excitement at the prospect of meeting Sir Gerald and finally discovering the exciting news he had imparted to the Vicar.

Six

'Miss Lawrence? Delighted to meet you. Come in. I've brewed some fresh coffee, which I'm sure you'll appreciate after your journey.'

Sir Gerald Taylor was not the man Belinda imagined him to be. In her mind's eye, Belinda had created a short stout figure with white hair and bushy sideburns, heavy jowls resplendent above a prominent stomach, much in the mould of the late Vicar. She saw him wearing thick-lensed glasses, a frayed tweedy jacket and having an effusive and pompous nature.

The man who met her at the door was the exact reverse of this. In fact, he was the perfect image of an idealised vicar, while the late Reverend Lawson could have been the role model for the absentminded untidy academic.

Tall and angular, Sir Gerald was a well-preserved man in his late sixties. Certainly his hair was grey but it showed no sign of receding or thinning. He reminded Belinda of a fit greyhound, muscular but trim and exuding energy. His bright eyes were inquisitive as though he sought information on everything that came before his gaze and computed that knowledge through a razor-sharp brain.

Alert and dashing, he was dressed in a sober jacket, well-pressed dark trousers and striped shirt snared at the collar by a conservative tie. Expensive Italian leather slippers shod his feet and his after-shave cologne radiated a fragrance that hailed from Jermyn Street.

His voice, when he greeted Belinda, was high but mellow and added to his charm.

'You must be fatigued after what I am certain was a tedious journey from Bath.'

Belinda was more than pleased to step into the book-lined living room, sink into a high-back leather chair and luxuriate in the warmth issuing from a comforting fire. The car ride to Winchester with Hazel had been less than enjoyable. Hazel was nursing a monumental hangover and not in the mood for company or discussing anything to do with the missing tapestry, so any comment Belinda made was greeted either by a snarl of annoyance or resentful silence.

They had travelled down in Belinda's car. She had dropped Hazel off at Itchen Abbas where she was to inspect the goods being offered by the recently bereaved family. Belinda arranged to meet her there later in the day.

'Firstly let me tell you how shocked I was to hear of the death of dear Arnold,' said Sir Gerald, in surprisingly exuberant tones.

Belinda stirred a spoonful of sugar into her coffee. 'Who?' Had there been another death?

'I refer to my old friend, Arnold Lawson. Your Vicar, I understand?' replied Sir Gerald, sinking into a chair opposite Belinda and crossing his long legs. A small hole in his black sock was revealed.

'Oh, yes.' Belinda realised how little she had known about the late Vicar. 'You were students together, I believe?'

Sir Gerald nodded. 'Cambridge,' he declared heartily, as though there could be no alternative. He sipped his coffee.

'Reverend Lawson told me that you were a great help to him over my piece of tapestry.'

Sir Gerald gave Belinda a startled look. 'He told you?'

'I mean, he left a message on my answering machine.'

Sir Gerald seemed to relax. 'I see. I wondered what you meant, because the police led me to believe –'

'The police? Have they been in contact with you?'

'Naturally.' A note of reservation crept into his voice. 'After all, Arnold had been staying with me and apparently I was the last person to see him alive.'

'But how did they locate you?'

'From his address book, it seems.'

Belinda wondered why she hadn't thought of that and wondered also why Inspector Jordan had not passed on that information. 'Of course,' she murmured.

Sir Gerald gave her a cautious look. 'What exactly did Arnold say in his message?'

'That you were a great help and that he had exciting news about the tapestry.'

Sir Gerald gave a soft smile and shook his head gently. 'Poor Arnold. He was always over-enthusiastic. I remember as a student he was forever getting carried away with undergraduate politics and obscure plans to change society. Even in his later years he was perpetually embracing extravagant proposals within the church. Women priests for example. Just imagine.'

Sir Gerald smirked into his coffee cup. Obviously the idea of female clergy cluttering up the vestry amused him.

Belinda's heart sank. 'Was he being over-enthusiastic about the tapestry?'

Sir Gerald smiled at her. 'I believe that he wanted it to be more than what it was, my dear.'

'And what exactly was, or should I say, is it?' Belinda asked, disappointment mounting.

Sir Gerald rose. Putting on a pair of half-moon reading glasses, he crossed to a desk and returned with a colour photograph. He handed it to Belinda. She took it and saw that it was a photograph of the tapestry.

'I took the liberty of photographing it as a matter of interest,' said Sir Gerald, taking his seat again and pouring a fresh cup of coffee.

'But haven't you got the tapestry itself?' Belinda felt a jolt of uncertainty.

Sir Gerald looked over the rim of his glasses. 'Oh, no my dear. Arnold took that back to Milford with him. He told me how anxious you where that it should be returned. That is why I took the photograph, as a reminder. A souvenir of a curiosity.' He waved the coffeepot at Belinda. 'Another cup?'

Belinda shook her head. She sank back into the chair and stared at the photograph in her hand. 'Then it *was* the reason.'

'The reason for what?' asked Sir Gerald, as he stirred his coffee.

'The reason he was murdered. You see, the tapestry wasn't found in the vicarage.'

Sir Gerald was thoughtful for a moment. He carefully placed the coffee cup down as though deliberating on what he was about to say. 'I think I should tell you exactly what I can about the tapestry.'

'Yes, please,' Belinda leant forward, not wanting to miss a word.

'It is an interesting piece. Quite unusual really, for a piece of domestic needlework.'

'Is it genuine?' asked Belinda, almost pleadingly.

'Genuine? Do you mean, is it a Norman work?' Belinda nodded hopefully. 'No, it's not Norman. Nor has it any connection with the Bayeux Tapestry, even though it portrays the coronation of William.'

Belinda gave a disappointed sigh. 'So it's only a Victorian copy after all.'

Sir Gerald shook his head. 'No, not Victorian. It is much earlier than that.'

'How much earlier?' Belinda was beginning to feel hopeful. All might not be lost.

'I would date it at early to mid-eighteenth century. Probably English and possibly executed here in Winchester. It is a remarkable copy. It recreates the stem stitch, as well as the laid and couched style used in the Bayeux work, and the wools employed in the stitching are uncannily similar to the original. Whoever worked it took great care to reproduce the style as close to the original as possible.'

'Why do you say it may have been made here in Winchester?'

'Just a hunch really.' Sir Gerald squirmed comfortably in his chair as he warmed to the subject. 'There is some speculation that the great original work itself may have been made here, or at least been influenced by the Winchester style of Anglo-Saxon art. The chief characteristic of that style is the placing of the central illustrated story within a frame or surrounding border.'

'You mean the objects at the top and bottom of the tapestry?' Belinda glanced down at the photograph and ran her finger along the ecclesiastical objects at the top of the embroidery.

'That is exactly what I mean,' said Sir Gerald, somewhat acidly. He turned a disdainful eye on Belinda. He was not used to explaining the obvious, but his interest in the subject under discussion soon overcame his irritation. 'But what defines it as being influenced by the Winchester style, is the fact that the borders are much more than merely ornamental. They're an integrated component in the storytelling. They comment upon the central theme or at least have a bearing upon it. An addendum if you like.' He gave a self-satisfied smile, pleased with himself and his knowledge.

Belinda opened her mouth to ask a question, but Sir Gerald was in full flight and he continued on, waving away the potential interruption to his erudite display.

'However, it seems more likely that the Bayeux Tapestry was crafted not here, but in Canterbury, or so current thinking would have it, even if it did absorb influences from Winchester.'

He paused for breath and Belinda, sensing a golden opportunity, took advantage of this lull in the flow of scholarly information. 'And my tapestry couldn't possibly be part of it? Of the Bayeux Tapestry, I mean?'

Sir Gerald glanced down at the fire and, grasping an ornate

poker, leant to stir the now sluggish coals. 'You are wasting my time, and yours, if you continue to delude yourself with that fiction,' he said curtly.

Hazel Whitby slammed the garden gate behind her and angrily surveyed the deserted street. 'A bloody waste of time,' she muttered venomously, casting a passionate glance back to the cottage. The decorous lace curtains quivered. The grieving family members were watching her departure. 'Idiots!' She glowed red with anger at the memory of the pitiful domestic objects the family had assembled for her inspection.

'Do you really expect to sell this rubbish?' she had demanded. 'It's not even worth sending to a junkyard. Far better to burn the lot.' She'd caught the shocked, offended gaze of the bereaved middle-aged couple, standing amidst their late mother's belongings. A twinge of conscience tweaked at her aching brain. *Surely you can be a little more gracious*, her conscience scolded. But Hazel's malevolent mood would not be disseminated. The cheap post-war furniture and commonplace E.P.N.S., which obviously had meant so much to the family, at least in emotional terms, held no value for her; this combined with rage at the wasted journey, along with anger at her own bad behaviour, fuelled her tantrum. With a withering glance and a snort of revulsion, she'd pushed her way up the narrow passage and out into the open street.

'What I need is a drink.'

As she and Belinda had driven into the village she'd noted the presence of a pub. Now she cast a sombre eye over a nearby stream and realised, with regret, that the pub was on the other side of the village. Energy would be required to reach it. And that was a scarce commodity. Hazel silently cursed her drinking partner of last night, conveniently forgetting that the onus was upon her when it came to her alcohol consumption. As she took a few tentative steps along the street her thumping head suggested to her that she should ease up on the gin and perhaps pursue a healthier lifestyle.

'Perhaps I should switch to vodka,' she speculated.

The prospect of continuing on without nourishment was a repulsive thought, so it was with some relief that Hazel came upon a nauseatingly rustic teashop. It consisted of a cottage, the front room of which had been converted into a tearoom, complete with chintz curtains and a collection of repulsive Toby jugs. A few weather-beaten outdoor tables and chairs were scattered about an untidy garden.

At this moment the sun burst from behind grey clouds. The thought of coffee taken in the unexpected warmth of the garden seemed irresistible.

Hazel sank down onto a damp chair and fumbled for her dark glasses as defence against the bright light. The door of the tearoom opened and a chubby woman, wearing a violent floral apron and a ferociously loveable expression, rocketed into the garden. She just managed to stop at Hazel's side before she collided with the mossy garden furniture.

'Tea, dear?'

'Coffee,' moaned Hazel, 'black.'

'Not until June, dear. Never serve coffee until June when the Americans start to arrive. Come by the busload they do.'

'Just for your coffee?' asked Hazel sourly.

The woman gave a guffaw that would not have been amiss in the repertoire of a pantomime dame and playfully shoved Hazel with such force that she almost fell from the chair. 'Get away with you. You are a tease. Although mind you, some of them say they have never tasted anything like my coffee.'

Hazel eyed the woman darkly. 'I'm sure.'

'So. Is it tea then? We have Assam, Darjeeling, Nilgiri, Ceylon, Lapsang Souchong, Gunpowder, Formosa Oolong, Earl Grey and Lady Londonderry.'

'No Typhoo Tea?' asked Hazel tartly.

The woman blanched at the concept and was at a loss for

words, a milestone in her life, Hazel was certain. 'Just strong black tea, I don't give a damn where it comes from – and dry toast,' she sighed in defeat. 'Oh, and some aspirin, if you have any.'

Widow Twanky, content now that she had a firm, if meagre, order, catapulted herself indoors. Hazel sank back in the seat and massaged her aching brow. Cigarettes had been on her list of no-no's ever since she'd read that tobacco smoke made your skin look like smoked haddock. This discouraging information, combined with the knowledge that several of her old school chums who had discovered the delights of tobacco smoking – along with the wizardry of masculine anatomy at roughly the same time and roughly the same place; the school changing rooms or the back row of the Odeon – had succumbed to emphysema or surgical extraction of one or both lungs. This had convinced Hazel that inhaling cigarette smoke was an unwise pastime.

She reminded herself of this conviction as she lit her cigarette. Drawing the blue cloud deep into her lungs, she gave such a raucous and enduring cough that the waitress feared she was about to lose her only customer for the day. Feeling marginally rehabilitated, Hazel relaxed in her chair and watched idly as a small black car slid to a halt opposite the garden.

A young man in a worn leather jacket, dark glasses and extensively shredded jeans stepped out. He bent to lock the car door. Hazel was captivated by the sight, especially at the glimpse of taut meaty buttock that flashed from beneath the ragged denim. The man turned, adjusted his dark glasses. With an impudent grin to Hazel, he sauntered over to the teashop.

Hazel gave an admiring sigh at his physical brashness. She smiled as the tiny silver cross hanging from his ear caught the late morning sunlight.

He drew closer.

'The most urgent political dilemma in 1064 was who should inherit the throne when Edward the Confessor died.' Sir Gerald strode out along the river path, his dark coat tails flapping behind him. A long woollen scarf snaked around his neck and cascaded over his determined shoulders.

When he had suggested to Belinda that she accompany him on his morning walk, she'd imagined a gentle stroll in the forecourt of the Cathedral. Or maybe a visit to Jane Austen's tomb. Instead, she found herself almost galloping in Sir Gerald's wake as he passed along St Swithin's Bridge, over the River Itchen, down Wharf Hill and upwards to St Catherine's Hill. She wondered if he was making an attempt on the world record in circumnavigating the city.

'But surely it would have been Edward's eldest son?' Belinda gasped.

'Not in those days,' replied Sir Gerald, almost running down a pair of lost and bewildered German tourists. 'Besides, the king had no issue. He was an ascetic, interested in the spirit. When he died there were four potential contenders for the throne.'

'Who were they?'

'Firstly, from Wessex – that is, from hereabouts – there was Edgar, the last prince of the Wessex Royal House.'

'You mean he was English?'

'To the bootstraps, as they say. His hereditary advantage was valid, but he had little influence or support and was readily passed over. Also waiting in the wings was the King of Norway, Harold Hardrada. His claim was based on his antecedent, King Canute, being the former ruler of Denmark as well as England.'

As they came to a sudden halt, a grateful Belinda asked, 'Didn't Canute try to stop the waves breaking on the shore?'

Sir Gerald glanced disparagingly at her before transferring his gaze to the city before them. 'The third aspirant was Harold Godwinson,' he continued, ignoring Belinda's interruption and striding forth once more. 'The Godwin clan had been a powerful force for twenty-odd years, so much so, they influenced the king as well as the church.'

'So Edward was forced to name him his successor?' said Belinda fretfully. A small pebble had found its way into her shoe and she wiggled her foot to ease her discomfort. The shoes were designed for elegant indoors, not tramping the highways of Hampshire.

'Harold was ambitious, there's no doubt about that, but he had two things in his favour. Firstly, the king nominated Harold as his heir and secondly, he was picked to be king by the foremost Anglo-Saxon body, the Witan.'

'Witan?'

'The name given to an assembly of senior churchmen and eminent persons. The "in-crowd" of the time. They served to advise the king on legal and social problems. A powerful group.'

'So Harold had a watertight case.' Belinda leant against a lamppost and removed her shoe.

Sir Gerald stopped mid-stride and frowned impatiently as Belinda shook the shoe and freed the offending pebble. 'Not as far as the fourth claimant William, the Duke of Normandy was concerned,' he declared as they resumed their trek. 'William was the bastard son of Robert the Devil. His claim to the English throne was based on the rather uncertain belief that he shared a common Norman ancestor with the English King Edward. Also, he claimed that Edward had named him as his successor.'

'So both Harold and William made the same claim?'

'Correct. But William also claimed that Harold had earlier taken a sacred oath at Bayeux. That oath is portrayed in the Bayeux Tapestry.'

'What was the oath?'

'The Tapestry does not spell it out, but William claimed Harold swore to be his man in England and to support his claim to the English throne. There was also the suggestion that in return, William promised his daughter's hand in marriage to Harold.'

'William felt cheated? So he invaded when Harold became king?' Belinda was conscious that her legs were beginning to ache.

Sir Gerald stopped again at the site of the Miz-Maze and Belinda was pleased to see that even he appeared slightly puffed.

From the top of St Catherine's Hill, the city lay before them and from this vantage point, Belinda could just make out her car parked outside Sir Gerald's house. A mild depression overcame her as she saw the distant figure of a parking officer approach the car and realised helplessly that she had parked illegally.

'It's my belief,' said Sir Gerald, as he took several deep breaths, 'that no matter what, William was born to be a conqueror. He was autocratic and when guile failed, then force was used to bend quarrelsome people to his way of thinking.'

All very well, thought Belinda gloomily. Fascinating as the history was, it did nothing to explain the absence of her tapestry. It did however explain something about Charles Godwin. Could it be that he was a descendant of Harold? Aloud she said, 'Did King Harold's family die out with him?'

Sir Gerald gave her a startled look. For a moment she saw something else in his eyes. Distrust? Wariness? Abruptly he turned on his heel and resumed his walk.

'My dear young woman,' he flung acidly over his shoulder, 'how do you expect me to know that?'

Belinda followed thoughtfully. She was not convinced that he was telling all he knew about the Godwin clan.

The trip to Winchester had been disappointing. Not only had she not recovered her tapestry, Belinda had learnt very little of importance from Sir Gerald.

At least she had a photograph of her tapestry.

That and a parking ticket.

After leaving Sir Gerald, who had reverted to his previous charming self and offered profuse apologies that he could not be more forthcoming over the whereabouts of the tapestry, Belinda slowed her car at a pedestrian crossing. Her mind was filled with a multitude of thoughts. Much of what she'd heard from Sir Gerald seemed superfluous, particularly when she had to face up to the fact that her tapestry had probably been the cause of the Vicar's death.

A gaggle of elderly ladies took their time in crossing the road. Belinda's gaze flicked towards the railway station. A train had just departed after disgorging its passengers. She watched idly as the hodgepodge of travellers found their way down onto City Road. Her attention was taken by a woman with a blonde ponytail hurrying determinedly through the crowd. She was dressed in a belted raincoat and kept her eyes downcast.

There was something familiar about the woman, and Belinda twisted around to follow the woman's progress down Sussex Street. As the woman paused at the gutter, she turned her head and Belinda saw, with a shock, that it was Mrs Godwin.

What was she doing in Winchester?

The road was now clear and Belinda drove off to collect Hazel. As she turned onto the road that took her to Itchen Abbas, she reasoned that there was nothing to prevent Mrs Godwin visiting the historical town. It was probably coincidental that they were there on the same day. Belinda put the matter out of her mind. After all, she had more important things to worry about.

Hazel opened the door. Clutched in her hand was the ubiquitous glass of gin, but it was the blackening eye and the bloodstained dress that shocked Belinda.

As arranged, Belinda had driven back to Itchen Abbas in search of Hazel. An exploration of the pub, being the logical first choice, revealed nothing, nor did the mourning family Hazel had visited. Indeed, Belinda got the distinct impression that if they ever saw "that rude woman" again it would be too soon.

Belinda wondered, not for the first time, how Hazel's brusque manner ever helped her achieve a sale.

Now, as she anxiously followed Hazel into her flat, these thoughts vanished in the face of this new dramatic situation.

'Stop fussing. I'm all right. Really,' growled Hazel as she sank onto the sofa and swigged her drink.

'You look like hell.' Belinda sat opposite her. 'That eye is getting blacker by the minute.'

Hazel raised a tentative hand and gently touched her bruised face. 'I must be losing my touch. I wouldn't have taken him for a basher, the bastard.'

Belinda looked around the room. It was obvious from the upturned furniture someone had been searching the flat. But for what? Hazel's jewellery? 'Where did you pick up – I mean meet him?'

'At that god-forsaken village. I didn't know how long it'd be before you came to collect me. He offered me a lift home, and I thought why not? I invited him in for a drink.'

Belinda raised an eyebrow. 'A drink?'

'Yes,' snapped Hazel. 'A drink. He'd been kind enough to drive me home. It was the least I could do.'

'The least.' Belinda smiled sardonically.

Hazel ignored her implication. 'We came up here. I started to pour a drink – then he hit me.'

Belinda looked down at the blood on Hazel's dress. 'But you've been bleeding. Have you got a cut?'

Hazel withdrew fastidious hands away from the blood-splattered fabric. 'No. I rather think that came from him. After he hit me, I remember reaching out and grabbing hold of his head. He pushed me away. As I fell I heard him scream and saw blood gushing down his face. I must have hit my head on the edge of the bar and passed out for a bit. When I came too, he'd gone, so I poured myself a drink – and then you arrived.'

'He must've left just before I got here.' Belinda rose and walked to the window. Weak sunlight filtered in through the curtains and something bright and shiny on the carpet caught her eye. She dropped to her knees and picked up the small glittering object. It was a blood-stained earring. A small silver cross.

Seven

'Brother Saul!'

Hazel lowered her glass and gave Belinda a disbelieving look.

'Brother who?'

Belinda dangled the small cross in front of Hazel.

'Saul! He wears an earring like this!'

'Do you mean to say you know the bastard?'

'I'm willing to bet I do! He's a member of that religious group in Norton St Philip. He's a monk, or at least pretends to be!'

Hazel retreated further into the sofa. 'Not the monks again? I thought you were over all that?'

'He goes under the name of Saul,' continued Belinda excitedly, 'although I'm sure that's not his real name. He belongs to the Fellowship of St Augustine. And what's more, he's the one I saw at Kidbrooke House!'

Hazel put her hand up to stop Belinda.

'Leave off, Bel! It's all too much for me to take in.' She put down her glass and held her throbbing head. 'Besides, my head feels as though Quasimodo's in there swinging from a million church bells.'

Belinda moved quickly to her side. 'Hazel, I'm sorry! Here I've been babbling on like an idiot, when I should've realised you needed to see a doctor. We should ring the police as well.'

'No!' Hazel took her by the arm. 'Not the police. It was my own stupid fault in accepting the lift from a stranger, and even more moronic of me to invite him in as I did.'

Belinda looked around the jumbled apartment. 'But he wrecked your flat! Besides, he could have killed you!'

'I know you think he's a killer, but he didn't kill *me*! So let's leave it at that. I'll see the doctor. I'll tell him I had one too many gins and fell over. He'll believe that – or at least pretend to. It wouldn't be the first time he's had to patch me up. But no police!'

'Did he take anything?'

'Some money from my purse, that's all. Luckily, he didn't find my credit cards.'

'I don't think he was looking for them,' murmured Belinda. 'At a guess I'd say he was looking for –'

'That bloody tapestry!' Hazel interjected angrily.

Belinda glanced down at the blood on Hazel's dress. 'If I were you I'd get out of that dress. These days you can't be too careful.'

A look of distaste passed over Hazel's face. She rose unsteadily and began to pull off the soiled dress, avoiding touching the bloodstains.

'I'll take you to the doctor's,' said Belinda as she stood. She ran the silver earring under the tap at the bar and washed her own hands. 'You know, if this does belong to Saul, it raises a disturbing question.'

Hazel made her way erratically to the bedroom and began to pull on a fresh dress. Belinda followed her, dropping the earring into her bag. 'How did he know you were in Itchen Abbas?' She paused at the bedroom door. 'Unless …'

Hazel's head popped out of the top of the dress. 'Unless what?' she asked in a startled voice. Her worried eyes demanded a reassuring answer, but there was little consolation in Belinda's response.

'Unless he's been following us!'

'He would have bled like a stuck pig if you'd torn this from his ear.' Mark dropped the silver earring onto the coffee table. He threw another log on the fire before sitting opposite Belinda and Hazel. Curled up at either end of the sofa, the two women looked like unmatched bookends. Outside, a few flakes of snow tumbled from the evening sky. The village of Milford settled down for the night, snug and warm against the chill darkness.

'Anyway, I think you're much safer staying here at the cottage with Belinda, particularly until you are over the concussion.'

'*Slight* concussion,' muttered Hazel pugnaciously.

Mark ignored her interruption. 'I can check on your flat each day and bring you any mail. We both think you should stay away from there for a time until we can sort this thing out.'

Belinda nodded in agreement. Hazel glanced from one to the other. 'You mean, you both want to keep an eye on me and make sure I don't make a damned fool of myself again!'

'That's not true.' Belinda decided that a small white lie was the safest course. Mark was not so restrained.

'Yes, it is. But we're also concerned for your safety. In fact, I'm concerned for both of you.' He gave Belinda a troubled look.

Belinda smiled. 'Thanks, Mark, but I can look after myself. Meanwhile the first thing to do is to check on Brother Saul's earlobe. If it's been bleeding, then he's our man.'

'And if he is, what then?' Mark asked impatiently. 'All it'd prove is that he beat up Hazel.'

'Which is a mere diversion,' Hazel said sardonically.

'There's nothing that ties him into actually murdering anyone.'

'Mark,' snapped Belinda irritably, 'he was at Kidbrooke House the day of the murder. The old man there had his eye gouged out and his thigh slashed open. The Vicar was murdered in the same way.'

'Agreed, they died in the same manner, but that's all!'

'But ...' began Belinda.

'But nothing,' interrupted Mark. 'OK, you saw him at the scene of the first murder. You've no evidence that he committed that crime. No evidence to connect him with the Vicar's murder either. I keep telling you, we've got to get positive proof.'

Belinda pursed her lips in annoyance and frustration.

Hazel raised herself on the sofa and made herself more

comfortable. 'There are a few things you're both overlooking. For example, how the Godwins fit into the scheme of things. From what you tell me Bel, they seem obsessed with this dead King Harold; and someone carved his name all over my very expensive table. The odds are that the Godwins did it when they couldn't find the tapestry among the things I'd bought at Kidbrooke House.'

'Why would they do that?' asked Mark.

'Pique!' snapped Hazel, annoyed at being interrupted. 'Which brings me to the second point. Exactly why would anyone want to steal your, apparently, worthless piece of tapestry?' Belinda shrugged in puzzlement. Hazel continued. 'And if it's true, as you believe, that Brother Saul murdered old de Montwhatever ...'

'Montfort,' muttered Belinda mechanically.

'... and then proceeded to bump off the Vicar, then I ask – with what purpose?'

'What do you mean?' asked Mark.

'Well, if both men were killed by this so-called Saul, in an attempt to lay his hands on the tapestry, then why on earth did he rummage through my flat today?'

'You said to find the –'

'I know what I said,' cried Hazel brusquely, 'but think, girl. Think! You say Sir Gerald claims the tapestry was returned with the Vicar.' Belinda nodded. 'And you believe the tapestry was stolen by the Vicar's murderer!'

Belinda sat erect. 'Of course! If Saul had stolen it from the vicarage, why would he be looking for it in your flat?'

'Assuming he was,' said Mark questioningly.

'That's right,' Hazel answered Belinda, ignoring Mark's interjection. 'And that means he is still searching for it. Therefore, that raises the question – did he murder the Vicar?'

'Well if he didn't, who did?' Belinda asked in bewilderment.

'One thing at a time,' retorted Hazel defensively. 'All I'm suggesting at the moment, is that the tapestry is still missing and Brother Saul's looking for it!'

'That means there is another murderer floating around, and they have the tapestry!' said Belinda.

'Which brings us back to the Godwins again,' said Hazel, looking like the cat who'd got the cream. 'It's possible *they* did the Vicar in!'

Mark looked thoughtful. 'But if Saul works for them, why is he still searching for the tapestry? Surely if the Godwins killed the Vicar, wouldn't they have taken it after murdering him?'

Belinda rose and stood with her back to the fire. 'That's assuming that the Vicar brought the tapestry with him when he returned from Winchester!'

Mark looked at her. 'But you said he did!'

'*Sir Gerald* said he did!' corrected Belinda.

'Do you think he's lying?' said Hazel, twisting around to confront her.

Belinda thought for a moment. 'No ... No, can't say that I do. It's just ...'

'Just what?' Mark reached out and took hold of her hand.

'Well, why would he? And the Vicar's message on the answering machine said he had something exciting to tell me!'

'But he didn't actually say that he had the tapestry with him?'

Belinda shook her head in disappointment. 'No, he didn't, but I'd asked him to return it to me. I just assumed that he had it with him at the Vicarage.'

Hazel wriggled to make herself more comfortable. 'What I don't understand is, why all this fuss over a scrap of tapestry? Your Sir Gerald says that it has no real value. He says it's eighteenth century and not worth much. So why is everyone getting their knickers in a twist?'

Belinda sighed. It was all getting too confusing. 'If I knew the answer to that ...' She left the statement unfinished. There was a brief silence with all three wrapped in their own thoughts.

'Either way,' said Belinda suddenly, breaking the stillness, 'even though I have no proof about Saul being a murderer, I'm convinced that he attacked Hazel. He's been following us, and for some reason decided to assault her.' Her voice grew strong with resolution. 'Tomorrow I'll go to the commune and see if Saul has an injured ear. That at least will prove something.' She turned to Mark. 'Since you were able to get information about Sir Gerald, I'd like you to do some more detective work.'

'What do you need to know, Holmes?'

Belinda smiled at him. 'Watson, I'd like to find out more about Sir Gerald, the Vicar and the Godwins.'

'Such as?'

Belinda threw her hands in the air. 'I wish I knew! But anything you can find out about them. The Vicar and Sir Gerald were at university together. Find out about their backgrounds, their interests, anything that you can. The same goes for Godwin and his wife. They said they'd just returned to England. From where? And why? Anything you can discover may be of help. In the meantime, I'm supposed to be continuing my "religious initiation" so I'll confront the Godwins myself tomorrow!'

Driving through the main street at Norton St Philip on her way to the religious commune, Belinda found her mind going over the events of the past days. She was annoyed that she herself hadn't realised that whoever murdered the Vicar would probably have the tapestry. So if Saul was still hunting for it, then it stood to reason that he was not the murderer. But even as she thought it, the suspicion that Saul was guilty of two murders strengthened.

Was he acting under instructions from the Godwins? It seemed unlikely that he would act on his own initiative.

And what was the value of the tapestry to them? Again the question haunted her.

She parked her car at the gate to the farm and began to walk down the deserted field towards the house. There was an eerie silence about the farm and Belinda was surprised by the absence of workers in the vegetable gardens. Pushing open the heavy wooden door, she stepped into the entrance hall. The silence was nerve-wracking. On her previous visits Belinda had noticed the muffled activities of the commune members as they went about their duties. Even in the chapel, there had been distant footsteps and the squeaking and clicking of doors opening and closing. Now this muted hubbub was missing and a strange stillness fell like a mantle over the ancient building.

Belinda's footsteps echoed across the bare vestibule as she made her way to Godwin's office. Peering around the door she saw that the room was empty.

On the cluttered desk there was a pile of scattered documents. Glancing over her shoulder to ensure that no one had suddenly appeared behind her, she moved across the room and inspected the papers.

They were rough black and white photocopies of sections of the Bayeux Tapestry.

Curiously, one particular portion had been duplicated several times. Belinda lifted these up for closer inspection. The photocopies showed two men half-kneeling beside what appeared to be a church. A Latin inscription was worked above – HAM ECCLESIA. One photocopy had some handwritten notes scribbled along the border.

"A 36 Dicul o/n shampton 27 a or m?"

'What on earth can that mean?' Belinda muttered under her breath.

In the distance a door slammed shut. Belinda jumped in fright.

The sound echoed unremittingly in the empty house.

The slap, slap of leather sandals on bare boards vibrated in the hall, first faintly, then increasing in volume. They drew near to the door.

Belinda held her breath.

If it was Godwin, she did not think he would appreciate finding her rummaging through his personal papers. Desperately she wracked her brain to dredge up a plausible excuse for being in his study.

After a moment of tension she breathed a slow sigh of relief as the footsteps passed by and receded into the outer reaches of the dormant house.

Anxious now to quit the study before being discovered, Belinda swiftly folded the photocopy and slipped it into her pocket. Holding her breath, she crept back to the entrance hall and peered around the door. All was quiet as before but, as the slamming door indicated, there was a human presence in the building.

Moving along the hall Belinda entered the chapel. It too was deserted. The faint smell of stale incense permeated the still air. The loaf of bread remained on the altar. By now the grey green mould had spread and covered more than half of the loaf.

A faint sigh drifted through the lifeless atmosphere. Belinda turned quickly and glanced up at the small balcony. The door leading to the storeroom clicked shut.

Someone had been watching her!

Belinda hurried into the hall and down the dark passageway leading to the store.

She flung open the door.

Standing at the foot of the stairs with an open Bible in her hand was the girl, Marianne.

Marianne slowly raised her head and gave Belinda a preoccupied smile. 'May the grace of God …'

'Be with you,' concluded Belinda. 'Yes, I do know that. Can you tell me where everyone is?'

Marianne ran her eyes over the walls as though expecting to find an explanation written on them. 'Maybe down at the stream. Maybe in the fields.'

'There's no one in the fields and what would they be doing down at the stream?'

Marianne gave a coarse giggle. 'Skinny dipping!'

'In this weather?' challenged Belinda, 'Don't be daft.' At that moment Marianne looked very much as though she may *be* daft. She pursed her lips and rolled her eyes skywards.

'Well … maybe they're in the barns!' she said, twisting her body in a coy motion.

'What do they do in the barns?'

Marianne's giggle turned into a vulgar laugh. 'They sow the seed!'

'Sow the seed? In a barn?'

Marianne collapsed into a snickering heap. Belinda gave a sigh of irritation. 'Is Mr Godwin here?' she asked tightly. This convulsed Marianne and she guffawed loudly. Belinda was beginning to lose patience with the girl. 'Marianne! I've come to see Mr Godwin or his wife. Are they here?'

Marianne stopped laughing long enough to catch her breath. 'Lord, no! Don't you know? The Master and Mistress are with the Holy Trinity!' Sniggers again engulfed her.

Belinda stared at the girl. She had previously wondered if the girl was simple but now began to think, at the moment, she was doped. Marianne sank into a stupor muttering unintelligible sentences. With a frown, Belinda strode back to the hall and out through the kitchen.

Crossing the cobble-stoned yard that separated the house from the barn, she became aware of distinctly unreligious music. Strident heavy metal music issued from the barn's wooden structure. Belinda stepped silently into the darkened interior. The corrosive odour of marijuana saturated the air and turned Belinda's stomach.

What soft winter light found its crafty way in cast a nebulous glow over the bales of hay. Searching out her path with tentative steps, Belinda edged into the shadowy barn. High above, the arched roof supports, such as those in a cathedral, suggested a religious aura but the barnyard odours created a distinctly earthbound reality.

A human wail of intense pleasure cut through the shrill music. Belinda echoed the cry, but in her case it was from shock. In a writhing group the young men and women of the commune were in an orgy of sexual animation.

Nearest to her, she saw Saul and his girl. As he arched back in a spasm of delight she saw that his earlobe was sheathed in a bloodstained bandage. Saul, sensing an observer, eased his head around. His eyes softly focused on Belinda. For a moment the two looked at each other. A slow lurid smile spread on Saul's lips. He eased himself away from the girl, presenting his naked self to Belinda. He held his hand out in a mock welcoming gesture.

Belinda, with a snort of disgust, turned and with speedy steps retraced her path. As she hurried to her car she heard Saul's mocking laughter.

'Well! While the cat's away the mice certainly do play!' Hazel paused in applying makeup to her bruised cheek. She had filled in the day attempting to disguise her black eye, so that it resembled less a piece of raw venison and bore some similarity to the surrounding flesh. It had not been a successful experiment. This, along with the doctor's recommendation that she refrain from alcohol until cured of concussion, had not improved her disposition.

Belinda flung herself down onto the sofa. 'And there is proof positive that it was Saul who attacked you. His earlobe had been bleeding badly.'

'I suppose I should count myself lucky that he only gave me a black eye. From what you tell me about his activities, it could have been a lot worse.' Hazel shrugged and sadly challenged her mirror. 'I suppose he is not turned on by old boilers.'

'Stop feeling sorry for yourself. But, yes. I do think you were lucky he didn't attempt anything else.'

'Has it occurred to you that the whole thing may have been a put-up job?' Hazel turned to face her.

'In what way? You mean, he wasn't looking for the tapestry?'

'Hmmm,' Hazel nodded thoughtfully. 'Perhaps it was meant to look like he was searching the flat for it.'

Belinda considered this new thought. 'In an attempt to make it look as though it was still missing and take any suspicion away from the Godwins, you mean? Assuming they have it?'

Hazel raised her eyebrows in agreement, but gave a squeal of pain and raised a tender hand to soothe her bruised cheek.

Belinda gave a sigh. 'Well, it's as good a theory as any other we've come up with.' She went into the kitchen and filled the kettle to make tea. Hazel meandered after her.

'Another mystery is, where were the Godwins today?' Belinda swilled warm water in the teapot. 'He was supposed to be there to instruct me. Do you suppose the shenanigans in the barn happen each time they leave the farm?'

Hazel smirked. 'Perhaps they happen all the time, even when Godwin is there.'

Belinda nodded. If that was the case why have the pseudo religious front? Why not just admit they were into group sex? She spooned the tealeaves into the warm pot.

'And what do you think the girl meant when she said the Godwins were "with the Holy Trinity"?'

'That they were dead?' suggested Hazel, with more than a hint of hope in her voice.

'No.' Belinda poured the hot water. 'I don't think we've heard the last of them – unfortunately.'

Hazel opened a packet of biscuits as Belinda carried the tray into the sitting room. Settling back, Belinda reached into her pocket and withdrew the photocopy she had taken from Godwin's office. She unfolded it onto the coffee table.

'What's that?' demanded Hazel, through a barrier of biscuit and tea.

'I found this on Godwin's desk. It's a copy of part of the Bayeux Tapestry.'

Hazel tentatively rolled her eyes. She was surprised that they did not hurt and so she rolled them again, this time more dramatically. 'Oh, not that again. I've had it up to the neck with that bloody thing.'

Belinda was studying the photocopy. 'Be quiet, Hazel. There's something familiar about this.'

Hazel snorted and reached for another biscuit. 'I'm not surprised. You've seen the thing often enough.'

Belinda continued to inspect the illustration. 'No, it's not that. It seems the same and yet ... different.'

'You don't have any Irish blood in you, by any chance?' sneered Hazel. 'The same, yet different. I ask you?'

Belinda turned the page on its side. 'What do you make of this?' She pointed to the handwriting.

Hazel leaned forward and peered at the inscription. 'Gobbledegook,' she said dismissively.

Belinda shook her head in disagreement. 'It must mean something. Do you think it's code of some sort?'

Hazel swallowed the last of her biscuit and took a longer look at the writing. '"A 36 Dicul o/n shampton 27 a or m?" What on earth is a thirty-six Dicul? A car? Something like a nineteen-eighties DeLorean, do you suppose?' she asked flippantly.

Belinda looked at her blankly. 'What's a DeLorean?'

Hazel grimly reflected that Belinda had barely been out of kindergarten when that stainless steel debacle had taken place, a debacle – sadly all those years ago – that she recalled only too well. She hurriedly waved the subject away. 'Nothing. Forget it. So, you think it's a code? How does that help us?'

Belinda did not have a ready answer. But she sensed that if decoded, the cipher would lead to the tapestry. Perhaps even reveal its mystery.

Eight

Belinda was sitting at the desk in Charles Godwin's office. On the desktop was a pile of colour photographs. Some were of the Bayeux Tapestry, others, pornographic snapshots of Saul and his girl. She was shuffling through them, searching for something, but try as she might, she could not find it.

In the distance came the distorted sounds of hymns intermingled with caustic rock music.

The Reverend Lawson moved towards her. 'Remember, Canterbury was rebellious and distrusted Odo.'

Belinda nodded. 'I remember. You told me that before.'

It was then that she realised the Vicar's eye socket was nothing but a grisly, gaping black cavity. Brother Saul stood beside the Vicar wielding a bloodstained knife. He moved closer to Belinda. She felt trapped in her chair and shrank away from him. She tried to call out to Mark for help, but no sound escaped her lips.

Suddenly, she realised that the threatening knife was no longer held by Saul.

The knife came closer and closer to her eye, but she could not make out the shadowy figure approaching her. She fought to recognise her assailant but the shape grew more obscure. The only object that she could focus upon was the sharp tip of the oncoming blade.

With a sudden lunge the aggressor thrust it into her eye.

Belinda screamed. She was amazed to find herself in her own bedroom. Her nightmare shriek echoed in her ears, loud in the silence of her cottage. Fighting to catch her breath, she pulled the perspiration soaked nightgown from her breast.

In the stillness of the night she could hear a faint snore from

Hazel's room, followed by the odd cry of a night bird, distant and lonely. She glanced at the bedside clock.

It was 2:00 a.m. Pulling on her dressing gown, she tiptoed downstairs. The aged timber creaked and grumbled at this nocturnal activity. The disturbing dream still seemed more substantial than the reality surrounding her.

The embers of the living-room fire needed only a few twigs to get a blaze going again. She sank down before its warmth. The rational world was returning yet the words the Vicar had spoken in her dream came back as loudly as if he had stated them again. Belinda mouthed the words to herself.

'Canterbury was rebellious and distrusted Odo.'

Yes, she thought. *William the Conqueror's brother, Odo, was made the Earl of Kent. He was charged with stealing the treasures from the churches.*

'And Sir Gerald said the Bayeux Tapestry was made in Canterbury, in Kent.'

Belinda had spoken aloud as a frisson of excitement overcame her. She sensed that here was a clue, a clue that would lead on to others.

The book of the Bayeux Tapestry, which she had borrowed from Mark, lay on the coffee table. She reached over and opened it up at the first illustration. It showed Edward the Confessor in his palace with Harold. This was followed by Harold and his men riding on horseback. Belinda turned the page to the third picture.

Her eyes widened in surprise.

It was the same as Godwin's photocopy.

Belinda took the copy and put it beside the book. She could now see that it completed the previous picture. The Latin text at the top of the photocopy was only part of the writing.

What appeared there read: HAM:ECCLESIA.

But when put with the previous picture the full Latin text read– HAROLD DVX:ANGLORVM:ET SVI MILITES: EQVI TANT:AD BOSHAM:ECCLESIA

'Bosham,' whispered Belinda softly, reading the English translation below, 'Harold travelled to a church in a place called Bosham.'

She gave a shiver, not from the cold night air, but from the sudden realisation that the church depicted in the book was the exact same church portrayed in her tapestry. She took the colour photograph that Sir Gerald had given her and placed it next to the book.

The churches were identical.

Out of the corner of her eye she was aware of a sudden movement. Turning sharply, she caught her breath in fright. There was a white shape at the door!

A baleful penetrating voice filled the room. '*Are you trying to give me a heart attack?*' Hazel stood in the doorway, a heavy brass candlestick held defensively before her. 'You don't know how close you were to being bopped on the head, Missy.'

Belinda gave a sob of relief. Hazel swept into the room and headed for the gin bottle.

'Damn the doctor. I need a drink. My nerves are in shreds. I heard someone moving about the house and thought your bastard monk was paying another visit.'

Belinda fell back onto the sofa. 'You can pour me one too. My nerves aren't exactly made of iron. The sight of you standing there in your nightgown is enough to frighten anyone.'

'Thank you, my dear. I think you're cute too,' muttered Hazel cattily, as she handed Belinda her drink. Both women took a healthy swig. They grasped the moment to retrieve their composure.

'May I ask what you're doing down here in the middle of the night?' said Hazel, as she sat beside Belinda.

Belinda hurriedly spread the book, the photocopy and the colour photograph out before her. In an eager voice explained what she had discovered.

'Bosham?' queried Hazel meditatively. 'It rings a bell

somewhere.' She sipped her poison. 'I've heard of it, but can't recall where it is.'

Belinda placed the photograph of her tapestry next to the book. 'The other extraordinary thing is that the church at Bosham, in the Bayeux Tapestry, is exactly the same as the one depicted in my tapestry. It shows William the Conqueror being crowned in that church.'

'Sweetheart, the kings of England are crowned in Westminster Abbey. Have been for centuries.' Hazel reached for the book and flipped though the pages until she came to the picture of Edward's burial and Harold's coronation. 'See. The abbey is totally different to your tapestry.'

They were indeed. There was no doubt that the abbey was more ornate.

'But mine is definitely the church at Bosham. They're identical. Why would it show William being crowned there? And I had a dream tonight. A nightmare about the Vicar. Then someone was going to kill me. In the same way. Stabbed in the eye.'

Hazel gave a shudder. 'I thought from the beginning there was something evil about that tapestry.'

Belinda rose and paced the room. 'The tapestry can't be evil but whoever murdered to get hold of it is. And what's its value? What is so important about it that they would kill to own it?'

'Who knows? It's not as though it's part of the Bayeux Tapestry.'

Belinda paused in her stride and turned to Hazel. 'But what if it is?'

Hazel gave a shrug of irritation. 'And what if I was the Queen of England?'

'No. I'm serious, Hazel.' Belinda hurried to the sofa and sat beside her. 'I know it's supposed to be worthless but if that's the case, why have there been two murders? Why were you bashed? Imagine for a moment – if it is part of the Bayeux Tapestry, how much it would be worth?'

'But your expert – Sir Gerald – he said it was an eighteenth century replica.'

'Supposing he lied?'

'*Is* part of the Bayeux Tapestry missing?' asked Hazel, her voice rich with doubt.

'It ends suddenly with the English escaping from the Normans.' Belinda was now pink with excitement. 'My tapestry could be the final panel, the end of the story. William's coronation as king of England.'

Hazel waved her gin at the colour photograph of the tapestry. 'But he wasn't crowned in this church at Bosham.'

Belinda gave a moan of frustration and collapsed back against the cushions.

'However, you raise an- interesting point,' said Hazel in a consolatory voice. 'If, as you say, two men were killed in order for someone to own it, then there must indeed be some particular value to it.'

Belinda sat forward on the sofa. 'The Godwins are obsessed with King Harold. They must know the value – and want it.'

Hazel picked up the photocopy and ran her finger along the handwritten notes. 'You may be right, Bel. If we could decipher what this writing means, it may give us a clue.'

The two women looked at the writing.

"A 36 Dicul o/n shampton 27 a or m."

'Well, if you ask me, it probably means the A36. The road.'

It was the following Saturday morning and Mark, who had been in Rome for the week, arrived fresh from the airport and demanded breakfast. Hazel elected to make the coffee, that being the least onerous task. Belinda made toast, cooked eggs and regaled Mark with the events of the past few days.

'Of course,' cried Belinda in delight.

Mark wolfed down another mouthful of scrambled eggs and poured a third cup of coffee.

Hazel, resentful that she hadn't thought of that obvious answer, was more critical. 'No one likes a smart arse, Mark.'

Mark flashed her an insincere smile that suggested that she knew exactly what she could do.

'How clever of you,' continued Belinda, glaring at Hazel, 'of course, the A36. That's near here, isn't it?'

Mark mumbled a 'yes' through buttered toast. He swallowed. 'It's the main road from here to Salisbury.'

'Where does it go then?' asked Hazel.

Mark inspected a jar of marmalade and scraped at the contents. 'Er ... on to Southampton, I think.'

Belinda waved the photocopy. 'That's it! That's what it means. Take the A36 to Southampton.'

'But what does "Dicul and 27 a or m" mean?' said Hazel. 'And why go to Southampton anyway?'

Mark finished piling marmalade onto his toast. With the sticky knife, he pointed to his briefcase. 'There's a road map in there.'

Belinda pulled the book from the case and searched for the A36. Her fingers followed the undulating line across the pages. 'Yes. It goes to Southampton.'

'But why?' Hazel repeated in frustration.

Mark poured what little coffee was left into his cup. 'What was the name of that place that Harold visited?'

'You mean where the church is?' Belinda reached for the book of the Tapestry.

'Bosham,' said Hazel confidently, 'but I can't recall where it is.'

'It's in Sussex,' replied Mark, equally confident, 'somewhere near Chichester. We've an office in Chichester and I'm sure there's a turn off from the main road that takes you there.'

'You're right,' confirmed Belinda, as she triumphantly located Bosham on the map. 'And,' she added excitedly, 'the A27 and the

M27 both lead to it from Southampton.' She·dropped the book and looked triumphantly at the others. 'It was instructions for the Godwins to find their way to Bosham.'

'According to the Tapestry, Harold prayed there prior to his sailing to Normandy,' Mark said, swallowing the last of his coffee.

'Do you know the church?' Belinda asked.

He shook his head. 'I've never been to the village. It's off the beaten track. Why would I go there?'

Belinda looked thoughtful. 'I wonder ...' She got to her feet and hurried into the long room at the back of the cottage where there was a large bookcase. Mark and Hazel lifted questioning eyebrows at each other.

Belinda reappeared with an armful of worn publications. 'Aunt Jane left a lot of old travel books.' She dropped to her knees in front of the fire and spread the books on the floor. Hazel leaned forward to pick one up.

'*The King's England*,' she said admiringly. 'Good old Arthur Mee. A modern Domesday Book. Modern in 1936, that is.'

Belinda was flipping through the book on Sussex. 'Here we are. Bosham. The Saxon chapel is the ancient church of the missionary, Dicul–'

'A missionary?' interrupted Hazel loudly.

'– Dicul,' continued Belinda, giving her an irritated glance, 'and is depicted in the Bayeux Tapestry, for in 1064 Harold, on his ill-fated journey to Normandy, prayed here in the Church of the Holy Trinity.' She dropped the book and looked at the others. 'That confirms it. The Godwins *were* with the Holy Trinity, as that fool of a girl said. And if it is of so much interest to them, I think we should investigate.'

That the Godwins, who were obsessed with King Harold, should visit a church that had some historic connection with the king

117

seemed understandable, Belinda reasoned with herself as she dressed the following morning.

Surprisingly, the sky was clear and there was the promise of a pleasant Sunday ahead. She made her way downstairs and began to brew a pot of tea. From upstairs came the stirrings of experimental activities, indicating that Hazel had risen at last, and was about to embark on the daunting prospect of facing a new day.

The kitchen phone rang. 'Are you awake?' Mark sounded sleepy.

Belinda stifled a yawn into the mouthpiece. 'Been up for hours,' she lied, 'just having breakfast.'

'I'll be there in an hour. Does Hazel *have* to come with us?'

'We had this out last night, Mark. We can't just leave her here. What if Saul showed up again? She's better off with us.'

Mark grunted. 'Well just make sure she's ready in time. Driving to Bosham is not my ideal way to spend a Sunday morning, and I'm not going to hang about waiting for her.'

Hazel finally emerged, but from the expression on her face Belinda knew that she could not expect any sensible conversation until much later in the day. Hazel was definitely not a morning person.

As she washed the breakfast dishes, Belinda heard Mark's car arrive and the beep of the horn – a summons she and Hazel were expected to respond to immediately.

Gathering her coat and bag she herded a sullen Hazel out and into the car. She was about to lock the house door when she stopped. 'Hang on, Mark. I forgot to switch on the answering machine.' She fumbled with the keys. Mark gave an irritated sigh.

'Leave the bloody thing.'

'Won't take a moment. Mum and Dad usually call on a Sunday.'

Mark and Hazel sat avoiding each others eye. Belinda hurried inside and pressed the answer button on the machine. The response was a vicious whirring noise, a garbled distorted announcement followed by a graunching noise. The machine came to a sudden stop.

'Damn!' snapped Belinda, cursing not only the machine but also her delay in replacing the faulty device. She flipped open the lid to extract the cassette and was faced with yards of magnetic tape that clogged the mechanism. She clawed at the ruined tape.

Mark tooted the car horn irritably.

'Oh, shut up Mark.' Belinda tore the last of the tape free. Disposing of it into the waste bin, she saw at the bottom, the old tape she had dropped there the night the Vicar died. Not having another new tape, she recovered the old one and gently placed it in the machine.

'I hope this will still work.' She metaphysically crossed her fingers and pressed the play button. Slowly the machine wowed into life.

With a shock she heard the Vicar's voice redeliver his message.

'I'm back from Winchester … er … that is … I mean I think we should talk as soon as possible. Sir Gerald was a wonderful help … and there is the most exciting news about your tapestry. Will you ring me? Er … What do I do now? … Er … that is all.'

Through the wowing voice, Belinda fought back a sob, suddenly reminded of the poor man's horrible death. The nightmare image of his bloodied body sprawled on the vicarage floor was as vivid as ever.

She reached across to rewind the tape, when there was a loud beep and the Vicar's voice was heard again in a second, previously unheard, message.

'Belinda. I forgot to tell … sorry, it's me again. I forgot to tell you, that you need have no fears about the safety of your tapestry. Sir Gerald is an expert and is used to handling things of this antiquity. He …'

The fluctuating voice ground to a basso profundo halt.

Belinda hit the machine.

Outside, the car horn bayed in elongated howls.

Belinda pressed the rewind button. The tape crawled backwards.

Her finger crushed the play button.

The Vicar's voice, careering from bass to castrato, repeated the message.

'... Sir Gerald is an expert and is used to handling things of this antiquity. He will take great care of it. He wished to spend more time examining it, so I ...'

Silence.

Belinda howled with suspense. Again she slowly rewound the tape and replayed it.

This time the tape slurred and vomited the voice out in unintelligible moans. Tears of frustration filled Belinda's eyes. With an almighty whack, she hit the machine. It gave an almost human wail. Instantly the Vicar's voice was clear and precise.

'He will take great care of it. He wished to spend more time examining it, so I left the tapestry with Sir Gerald in Winchester.'

Nine

Ignoring Hazel's whining at the inconvenience and Mark's irritation at the delay, Belinda dragged them back into the cottage to play the tape. Through the distortion they were able to grasp the meaning of the recorded call.

'He *lied*,' said Belinda, almost in triumph. 'Sir Gerald lied to me. He told me that the Vicar had the tapestry with him when he returned from Winchester. Yet the Vicar claims – or claimed – it was still with Sir Gerald.'

Belinda was reaching for the telephone when Mark put out a hand to stop her. 'Who are you ringing?'

'That lying Sir Gerald, who else?'

'But wait a minute,' said Mark, looking confused. 'How is it that you've just discovered the Vicar's message?'

Belinda had little time for explanations and began to dial Sir Gerald's number.

'He must have recorded two messages the night he died. I only heard the first one because this machine is old and the tape got damaged. I threw it in the waste bin. Today I had to salvage it, when the other tape was ruined. That's when I discovered there was a second message.'

She put up her hand to stop Mark's next question. 'It's ringing,' she said tensely.

There was an impatient silence in the cottage broken by the imperceptible sounds of Belinda's indignant breathing and the faint ringing tone of Sir Gerald's telephone. As the moments ticked by Belinda's impatience increased and her anger at Sir Gerald's deception gradually gave way to frustration. She realised there was to be no answer.

She slammed the phone down. 'The prick!' she bellowed.

Hazel's plucked eyebrows rose, not in surprise at Belinda's uncharacteristic expression, but in consummate agreement.

Belinda reached for her coat and hurried to the door. 'Come on. Let's go.'

'Where to?' muttered Hazel as she hauled herself from the sofa – hoping Belinda meant the nearest coffee shop.

Belinda paused at the door. 'To Winchester, of course.'

Mark snorted derisively. 'To an empty house? He's not at home, you know that and there's no way of knowing when he will be. So if you think I'm driving all the way to Winchester on a wild goose chase, then you've got another think coming.'

Hazel plopped back onto the sofa again. She might as well make herself comfortable until the two protagonists sorted themselves out.

'Wild goose chase?' Belinda flushed angrily. 'He lied to me, and I want to know why, *and* what he's done with my tapestry.'

'There's no point rushing off there until you know you can see him. In the meantime calm down. There may be a perfectly acceptable explanation,' replied Mark, with exasperating male reasoning.

Hazel cleared her throat sceptically. 'Just as there may be a perfectly acceptable explanation for the Vicar's murder.'

Belinda and Mark turned and met her critical stare.

The road to Southampton slithered beneath the tyres of Mark's car. The hum of wheels on bitumen invaded the interior of the vehicle as each occupant, though secured within, travelled along different personal highways.

To Belinda, seated in the front passenger seat, the passing trees could have been festooned with diamonds, the fields littered with gold bullion; it would have made little impact on her. The revelation that Sir Gerald had lied stunned her and her mind was a sea of speculation. Fidgeting with thwarted excitement at the delay in confronting him, she made up her mind to travel to Winchester at the first opportunity to challenge him. This visit to Bosham, which earlier had seemed full of intrigue, paled against the prospect of discovering the whereabouts of the tapestry. Not to mention, why Sir Gerald should have denied having it in his possession.

Mark, a grim expression on his handsome face, fingers tense on the steering wheel, drove resolutely. His eyes may have been on the road, but his mind digested the ramifications of the lie. There were so many diverse threads which, although he could not determine any pattern, he felt were all part of the same subject. All interconnected in some hidden framework.

Only Hazel, snug in the back seat, allowed her thoughts to be self-centred. She longed for a cup of strong black coffee.

Her remark about the Vicar haunted Belinda on the drive to Bosham. Hazel was right. If the tapestry had never returned with the Vicar, why was he murdered?

If it had been a break in that had gone wrong, or a drug related crime, why was he murdered in the exact same way as William de Montfort?

The only connecting link was the tapestry. And that, it seemed, was still in Winchester.

But where was Sir Gerald?

Several times during the journey Belinda had phoned him on her mobile phone, but each time there was only the repetitive lifeless ringing in acknowledgement of her call.

As the car made its approach into Southampton Belinda suddenly felt sick as the thought struck her that perhaps, just perhaps, Sir Gerald had been murdered too.

It was mid-afternoon when they arrived in Bosham. A coffee stop at Southampton, at the repeated insistence of Hazel, had delayed them further. Although a weak sun shone through hazy clouds, the chill breeze made them shiver as they stepped from the car. Wrapping their coats around them, they wandered down to the village that jutted out into an estuary of Chichester Harbour.

The conspicuous shingled broach spire of Holy Trinity acted as an usher in guiding them to the church. It stood at the top of a creek on the outskirts of the harbour. The dark waters of the creek reflected the buff coloured tower, while surrounding trees arranged fortified branches in a protective cocoon.

Hazel, more bad-tempered than before – the longed-for coffee had proved to be undrinkable – was determined to display her hostility. She plonked herself down on a seat overlooking the creek, resolutely turning her back on the church. Belinda and Mark, taking this to mean she no longer wished to take part in the afternoon's activities, stole away into the church grounds. Hazel was left to mouth mild obscenities at a duck that was unwise enough to waddle into her orbit.

The village radiated the established calm of an English Sunday afternoon. In the churchyard, even the birds seemed oddly secretive.

The interior of Holy Trinity was not only dim, but also glacial. Belinda pulled her coat tight about her neck as she stepped into the church, past the ancient wooden door and down worn steps. She pocketed a pamphlet detailing the history of the church. Mark lingered to read the notice board in the porch, but it held only times for choir practise prior to the approaching Christmas services, and he soon followed Belinda.

As their eyes became accustomed to the gloom, they could make out, on their right, a half wall, with steps leading down to an arched doorway. Raised about five feet above the steps was an open Gothic chapel, whose floor provided a ceiling for the crypt below.

'There must be a vault beneath the chapel,' whispered Mark in Belinda's ear, his chill breath sending a tremor down her spine.

'Do you think anyone's buried down there?' she asked, hoping the answer was a definite "no". To her discomfort Mark simply nodded a confirmation and moved nearer to the chancel. Feeling nervous, Belinda followed him. They stood looking towards the chancel arch where colourless sunbeams seeped in through the five-light east window.

Belinda gave a gasp of recognition. She fumbled in her coat pocket, drawing from it the crumpled photocopy of Harold Godwinson praying in this very church.

'Look. The arch. It's identical to the Bayeux Tapestry.'

Mark glanced at the photocopy. 'More stylised than identical,' he said academically, 'but you're right.' He ran his finger along the embroidered illustration. 'It's the same, even down to the horseshoe contour. That's rather unusual, I gather.'

'And it's the same as my tapestry. Which means it *does* show William being crowned king in this church.'

Mark shook his head. 'But we know he wasn't.'

'Oh, Mark,' said Belinda, climbing the ancient stone steps into the chancel, 'this is getting very weird. It must mean something. Is my tapestry part of the Bayeux original or a copy? If it's original, why show this church, when the king was crowned in Westminster Abbey? What's the connection?'

'And why kill for it?' asked Mark.

They were interrupted by the squeak of the church door as it opened. A small black figure entered and, humming a toneless rendition of a Bach cantata, made its way up the nave. At the steps leading up to the chancel, the figure stopped suddenly at the sight of Belinda and Mark.

They found themselves looking down onto the genteel features of an elderly man. Small, spindly, dressed entirely in black, he looked like a shrivelled crow. He peered from one to the other, eyes wide with surprise.

'Oh! You startled me. I thought all the Sunday trippers had gone.' His voice matched his appearance, sombre and crackly.

'I'm sorry,' said Belinda, 'should we leave?

The man's pallid features eased into a congenial smile. 'Good Heavens, no. We welcome visitors. You mustn't mind me. I play the organ. For my own edification, you understand. The Vicar wisely turns a blind eye, or should I say a deaf ear, to my musical transgressions. But he kindly lets me torment his organ, when it is not in use for liturgical purposes.'

Mark stifled a laugh, as Belinda surreptitiously kicked him in the shin. Unaware that he was providing much needed amusement for Mark, the man continued, 'I'd hoped to get some practise in before Evensong.' So saying he placed a pile of sheet music on the small organ and turned to his visitors. 'Do you know the history of Holy Trinity?' He seemed eager to air his knowledge.

'We know King Harold prayed here before travelling to Normandy,' said Mark, somewhat smugly.

The old man frowned. 'Hmmm, yes. 1064. When he was trapped into swearing allegiance to the Duke William of Normandy. Infamous creature.' He turned solemn eyes onto his captive audience. 'As you may imagine, we do not think highly of William in these parts. There are some of us who would prefer the Norman invasion had not taken place.' He wrinkled his nose as though he detected a bad odour. 'A barbarous lot. Descended from the Vikings, so what could you expect?' The question was clearly rhetorical, because he continued unremittingly. 'Replacing our language with French! And such dreadful slaughter. Why, even King Harold was butchered in the most appalling manner.'

Unquestionably, this was the crux of the matter, and it stuck in the old man's craw.

Belinda and Mark exchanged an amused glance.

But their muse was not to be distracted.

'Imagine deliberately blinding a man. Firing an arrow into his eye. Disgraceful.'

Belinda instantly recalled the image on the Bayeux Tapestry. 'He was blinded? Are you sure?' she demanded.

The man gave her a sharp look. 'Sure? Of course I'm sure. I thought every Englishman knew that.' He spoke as though he thought it more of a national duty, than a mere acceptance of an historical event. 'Mind you,' he added sceptically, 'there is a school of thought that has him dying from a leg wound.'

'Why would they believe that?' asked Mark.

'Because that's how Harold's death is depicted. There is some confusion as to exactly how he died. The Bayeux tapestry shows two figures, both purported to be Harold. As that is our only near contemporary record of events, we must assume it to be correct. There is a manuscript of indeterminate date – it may or may not be contemporary – which suggests that Harold was literally hacked to pieces. According to that version he lost his head, was stabbed in the chest and stomach, and his leg was cut off to be borne in triumph by the marauding Normans.'

'How horrible,' said Belinda.

'Mmmm,' agreed the man thoughtfully. 'I'm of the opinion that he sustained only one wound – that in the eye. The thigh-slashing episode I believe is most likely a token.'

'Of what?' asked Mark and Belinda, in unison.

'Castration!' declared the man with a certain relish. 'But getting back to the two figures, one has an arrow in his eye while the second, has his thigh is slashed open by a mounted Norman. Repairs to the Tapestry over time have resulted in different theories being put forward, such as Harold's blinding being a symbol. I don't agree with that view. William was given to blinding and castration as a punishment in preference to hanging. As I said, barbarous.'

Clearly hanging was not to be considered uncivilised in his view.

'No,' he continued heatedly, 'you can't tell me that it was symbolic. William wanted vengeance and took it in the most horrific way.' He paused for a moment, as though appalled at a recent event, not something that happened nearly a thousand years ago. He gave a disillusioned sigh. 'However, experts can't agree if both figures are meant to be Harold or only the second one.'

'So it's possible he could have been wounded both ways?'

The old man shrugged. 'We have no real proof either way.'

Belinda grasped Mark's arm. 'But that means whoever killed the two …' She had no need to continue, for Mark nodded his head in mute, but earnest, agreement.

'However, Harold is not the only claim to fame that we have,' continued the man, making his way into the nearby Gothic chapel.

Belinda and Mark followed him and gazed at the rough stone walls. Their guide took up a theatrical pose in front of the altar. He pointed with a dramatic finger to the floor of the chapel.

'Here, in All Hallows chapel, beneath our feet,' he proclaimed with a flurry of trumpets – which only he could hear – 'is the crypt which was the original monastic cell that served Dicul and his Irish monks in the seventh century.' He spread his arms in a wide embrace. 'This chapel, and indeed the church, is built upon their building, as well as their faith.'

Belinda glanced at the floor half expecting to see an open tomb beneath her feet. She shivered.

The old man, now in full flight in his role as local guide, walked to the iron barrier that overlooked the nave. 'Yes, this ancient building has many historic connections. It has been of great interest to archaeologists and the like, with many excavations over the years. They seem very taken with the huge stone sarcophaguses from ancient times.

'Formidable pieces they are, I'm told. Could crush a man if one was unlucky enough to have one fall upon them.' He gave an uncertain chuckle, as though vaguely amused by the idea. 'As recently as 1954, during an extensive dig, they unearthed an intriguing apsidal-headed coffin. When they opened it, it revealed the bones of a powerful giant of a man.'

He turned to Belinda and Mark and, after a dramatic pause, continued in a hoarse exaggerated whisper, 'They were the remains of the Earl Godwin of Wessex.'

A hush fell over the church as he closed his lips. Belinda, in spite of herself, felt the hairs on the back of her neck bristle.

Mark broke the silence. 'You mean, Harold's father?'

'The very same,' said the man, with a satisfied smile.

He walked across the Gothic chapel and stamped his foot on the stone floor, as though testing its strength. 'As a matter of fact, I believe there is to be a further excavation soon. Some expert from London is to burrow away, no doubt hoping to find further remains of Dicul and his monks.' He sounded as though he thought this activity a godless pastime. 'I should let them rest in peace,' he confided in a reverential whisper.

Belinda's fingers weakened their grip on the photocopy of the Bayeux Tapestry. It floated like a feather, to land at the feet of the old man. He stooped uneasily, wheezed, and picked it up. His eyebrows rose in surprise when he recognised it.

'Ah. The Bayeux interpretation of our beloved church.' He peered at Belinda and Mark. 'Are you members of the same group?'

Belinda and Mark looked at each other. 'What group?' asked Mark. Belinda felt she knew the answer.

'There was a small group here earlier this afternoon. Seemed very interested in Earl Godwin and Harold. I assumed they were from an historical society.'

Belinda felt her mouth go dry. 'What did they look like?'

'A middle-aged couple and a rather …' The man searched for the right expression, thought of it, and then decided that Christian charity demanded he temper his intolerance – after all, the House of God was not the place to use such expletives. 'Let me just say,' he continued in a disdainful voice, 'a rather undesirable youth. Torn clothing. Earrings. You know the sort.' His nose wrinkled in distaste.

'How long ago where they here?' asked Mark.

'Shortly before you, I should imagine,' said the old man, losing interest in the subject and making his way back to the organ. 'I saw them again in the church yard as I came in just now.'

Mark grasped Belinda's arm. 'Hazel!' he said urgently.

Pulling Belinda along with him, he ran down the nave. Together they burst into the churchyard. Mark, being first to clear the church, led the way. He headed towards the churchyard wall.

Belinda surprised herself with her agility, by leaping over a memorial stone and careering past the church. Her heels sank into the damp winter earth. She tried to fight down the rising panic in her breast. She imagined Hazel being confronted by Saul. Previously he had only beaten her. There was no way of knowing what he might do this time.

Racing through the low restraining limbs of the trees, they ran to the spot where they had left Hazel.

The seat was empty. Hazel had gone.

Ten

'You don't think she's gone off with him again, do you? With Saul?' Belinda looked at Mark. 'I mean of her own free will?'

They were on their way back to Milford and Hazel's disappearance weighed heavily on Belinda's mind. What sunshine there had been was now long gone and a stormy night added to Belinda's pessimism.

A thorough search of the churchyard and village had revealed nothing.

Hazel had simply vanished.

'You know my thoughts on Hazel,' replied Mark, as he accelerated to overtake another car. 'I've always believed that her preference for a bit of "rough" would get her into trouble one day, and this could be the day.'

That was exactly what Belinda did not want to hear. She had similar feelings. She was looking for consolation, not confirmation.

When it had become apparent that Hazel had simply not wandered off looking for coffee or taken an unlikely interest in the local antiquities, Mark decided that the police should be informed.

The police, while being helpful and polite, had taken the view that "perhaps the lady just accepted a lift home". Mark acquainted them with Hazel's disagreeable mood, which led to their suggestion that she'd simply got tired of waiting for Belinda and Mark to return, and had either taken a bus, or cadged a lift with some fellow travellers. They had taken copious notes on Hazel's appearance, but implied that there was probably nothing to worry about. Belinda would most likely find her waiting for them when they returned home.

But there was no sign of Hazel at the cottage.

Mark brought the car to a halt outside the garden gate. Belinda could tell from the gloomy unlit windows, that the house was empty. As she turned the key in the door and made her way into the warmth of the central heating, her remaining hope was that Hazel had elected to return to her own flat.

The unanswered ringing tone from Hazel's phone put paid to that forlorn hope. Belinda dropped the receiver into the cradle.

'Well, that's it. She's missing. We'd better call the police again.'

Mark was hesitant. 'Let's wait until morning. We've no proof that she didn't just go off of her own accord. If she's still not contacted you by then, by all means let's ring the police. After all, we don't want to end up with egg on our face if she turns up with a smile on hers.'

'But surely she wouldn't go with Saul after he'd beaten her up?'

'We don't know if she did go with him. We are just surmising it was him and the Godwins that the old man saw in the church.'

'Oh, it was them all right,' Belinda said vehemently.

Although Mark did not reply, he knew what Belinda claimed was probably accurate. Still, there could be a rational explanation. To act hastily might only result in embarrassment all around.

'Shall I stay tonight?' he inquired, slipping his arms around Belinda and drawing her close. Belinda held him tight. His strength seemed comforting as well as soothing. 'No. I'll be all right. Besides, I'd only keep you awake tonight. I don't think I'll get much sleep.' They kissed. Belinda again felt consolation in his embrace. She began to have second thoughts about sleeping alone, but rejected them when she realised that her anxieties would prove insurmountable. The prospect of a restless night loomed large.

At the door Mark kissed her again. 'I'll call you first thing in the morning.'

Belinda smiled her thanks and watched him make his way out

the garden gate. As she climbed the stairs to her bedroom, the sound of his departing car faded away into the darkness. The silence of the country night fell like a leaden blanket over her ears. She switched on the bedside radio for companionship. The delicate spirit of a Mozart piano sonata lifted her heart a little.

The prophecy of a troubled night proved more than accurate. When the grandfather clock in the hall wheezed before striking three, Belinda was to be found downstairs curled up on the sofa, a near empty brandy glass beside her, a worried frown on her brow. Outside a harsh wind had sprung up, driving the rain hard against the windows and rattling the shutters. The tap, tap of a branch against the windowpane added a pessimistic comment.

Belinda took a final sip of brandy. Her mind was full of speculative thoughts. As she pulled her dressing gown around her, she ran these once more through her head, in an attempt to formulate a plan of action.

For action, and vigorous action at that, was called for.

But what to do first?

There was the sudden disappearance of Hazel to contend with, assuming that she had indeed disappeared and not just gone off with a bit of "rough", as Mark suggested.

There was the mystery of the Godwins and what they were doing in Bosham.

The revelation of how King Harold was slaughtered and the similarity to the recent murders only confirmed her belief that Charles Godwin was involved.

And finally, the most fascinating puzzle, Sir Gerald's lie about the missing tapestry.

Each issue was intriguing – but which one to follow up first?

Belinda fell into an exhausted sleep, only to be roused by the persistent ringing of the telephone. She glanced at the clock and was startled to see that it was after nine.

'I've got some interesting news.' Mark's voice, sharp with excitement, crackled from the receiver. 'You remember my father was doing some detective work on Sir Gerald for us? Well, he rang this morning. It seems that not only was Sir Gerald at university with the Vicar, but also with William de Montfort.'

'You're joking?' cried Belinda.

'No way,' replied Mark, 'they had been great pals it seems, and what's more, Sir Gerald was a frequent visitor to Kidbrooke House in the old days.'

'So he would have known about the tapestry?' Belinda said excitedly.

'Not sure about that. It's possible of course, but the really sensational news is what Sir Gerald chose as the subject for his thesis.'

'What was that?'

'Nothing less than the Bayeux Tapestry and its iconography.'

Immediately after talking to Mark and instructing him to notify the police that Hazel was still missing, Belinda telephoned Sir Gerald, but the constant ringing confirmed that he was still not at home.

Either that, or he was not answering the phone.

Determined now to confront Sir Gerald with his lie, Belinda dressed hurriedly and set off for Winchester.

As the Godwins farm was on her route, Belinda decided to stop off at the commune. The shingle bearing the Gothic inscription, "Fellowship of St Augustine", swung to and fro in the blustery wind. Stepping from the car, Belinda's dark hair was whipped into Medusan locks. Folding her arms across her chest, she made her way towards the buildings.

As she neared the house, Belinda saw the distant figure of Mrs Godwin approach the barn from the back of the house. She knew her from the blonde ponytail that hung over the collar of her anorak.

Fighting against the squally wind, Belinda approached the barn. As she reached the door Mrs Godwin emerged. The two women cannoned into each other. Mrs Godwin gave a cry of fright and dropped a plate and tumbler she carried. The plate shattered and the plastic tumbler bounced once or twice before being whirled away in a violent gust of wind.

The woman glared angrily at Belinda. Fighting against the wind, she pushed the large barn door closed. With a grimace, she bolted the lock and leant defensively against the door. 'You've got a nerve,' she declared in her masculine voice. 'Sticky-nosing about the place like that.'

'I'm not sticky-nosing. I'm simply wondering why your husband wasn't here this past week?'

Mrs Godwin pushed a stray handful of hair off her brow. Defiantly she plunged her fists deep into her pockets. 'What's it got to do with you where he was?'

'Simply that he was to meet with me each day to instruct me in his religious beliefs.'

Mrs Godwin curled her lip in a disbelieving sneer. 'You've no interest in religion.'

'Oh? And what makes you say that?' Belinda said defiantly.

Mrs Godwin kicked the shattered plate. Pushing past Belinda, she began to walk swiftly back to the house. Belinda gave pursuit.

'I asked you a question. What makes you think I have no interest in the Fellowship?'

Mrs Godwin wheeled around to face her. There was a look of contempt and loathing in her expression that startled Belinda into silence. 'You know it's all a fake.' Mrs Godwin spat the accusation into Belinda's face.

For a moment the two women stared at each other. Then Mrs Godwin turned and, bursting into tears, ran into the house. Belinda stood bewildered. Yes, of course she thought the Fellowship a fake, but she little expected to hear Godwin's wife confirm it.

Now that Mrs Godwin was possibly in a mood to divulge further indiscretions, Belinda opened the door and stepped into the kitchen. One should strike while the iron is hot.

Mrs Godwin was seated at the large table with her head buried in her hands. She glanced up at Belinda and gave a hostile scowl. Belinda sat at the table opposite her.

'I'm sorry if I upset you,' she said softly. 'It's just that each day last week, when I came, there was no one here.'

Mrs Godwin sniffed, then wiped her nose on the back of her hand. 'You didn't come each day.'

How do you know that? Belinda wondered to herself.

Aloud she replied, 'Well, that's true. I did miss a few days, but there didn't seem to be any point coming, if Mr Godwin wasn't here.' There was no reply from Godwin's wife. With feigned innocence, Belinda continued, 'Marianne said you were with the Holy Trinity.'

At the mention of the girl's name, Mrs Godwin was suddenly alert. She glared at Belinda. 'That girl is a simpleton. You shouldn't take notice of anything she says.'

'I'll bear that in mind,' nodded Belinda. 'It's just that I was at Holy Trinity church in Bosham yesterday and I wondered if you'd been there?' Belinda hoped she sounded ingenuous. But from Mrs Godwin's expression she had reason to doubt it.

'You've been following us.' The accusation was direct and reproachful.

'Hardly. But you *were* at Bosham?'

Mrs Godwin avoided her eye. 'He still is. He's obsessed with it.' She sounded bewildered. More disappointed than angry.

'By "he", I assume you mean your husband?'

The woman glanced back at Belinda. Her eyes confirmed the question.

'And by "it" I take it you mean the religion?'

To her surprise, Mrs Godwin gave a disrespectful laugh. 'He believes in it less than you do.' The bitterness in her voice could not be disguised.

'If not the Fellowship, what then?'

Mrs Godwin ran her fingers back through her hair and adjusted the band holding her ponytail. 'He's obsessed with King Harold and the whole Norman Conquest.'

'Is that because he believes he's descended from the English kings?' Belinda's question astonished Mrs Godwin. For a moment she did not reply but only stared in disbelief at Belinda.

'You know about that?' she asked, in a soft incredulous voice.

Having gone this far, Belinda was uncertain how much she should reveal. After all, as angry with her husband as Mrs Godwin was now, there was no way of knowing if this was just a temporary spat. Plus there was the real danger, that if she hinted at what was suspected then she herself could be at risk. Saul worked with Godwin and as far as she was concerned, Saul could be a murderer. Belinda gave what she hoped was a nonchalant shrug.

'I know that Godwin was the family name for King Harold and that he was the last English king.' She grew bolder. She might as well as be hung for a sheep as a lamb. 'I also know that your husband was interested in a piece of tapestry that once belonged to Kidbrooke House in Yorkshire. You and he came to my cottage after the auction, with the express purpose of locating the tapestry.'

Mrs Godwin smirked. 'My, my. You have been an industrious little detective.'

Belinda ignored her jibe. 'He wants that tapestry, doesn't he? Why does he want it?'

Mrs Godwin gave an irritable sigh. 'He's been obsessed with it ever since his university days. He found some document that claimed there was a missing panel of the Bayeux Tapestry and he's determined to find it.'

'Which university did he attend?' Belinda asked. She'd already guessed the answer.

'Cambridge,' replied Mrs Godwin, still disapprovingly. 'That, combined with his obsession about his precious family tree, is enough to drive you mad.'

'Family tree?'

Mrs Godwin gestured towards the interior of the house. 'He's traced his family tree back to Henry Godwinson, and you're right. He thinks he's the legitimate King of England.'

Belinda choked back a laugh. 'You're not serious?'

'I'm not, but he is. That's the trouble. And now he wants to dig it up.'

Belinda's eyes widened a fraction. What did the woman mean? 'Dig what up?'

Mrs Godwin suddenly looked apprehensive, as though she had perhaps said too much. She toyed with an empty cup and saucer. 'I don't know,' she muttered evasively.

Belinda felt that she did indeed know, but realised, in her current resentful mood towards her husband, she had revealed more than she should. Sensing that she would get no further with that line of questioning, Belinda changed her approach.

'Yesterday, in Bosham, a friend of mine went missing.' She watched carefully for any reaction from Mrs Godwin and was rewarded by the look of alarm that crossed the woman's face. 'I don't suppose,' she continued guilelessly, 'that you would have seen her during your visit? Her name is Mrs Whitby. I think you know of her? She runs the antique shop in Wells, where there was a break in recently. Damage was done to a piece of furniture. Do you recall?'

Mrs Godwin gave a gasp and rose from the table. 'I have nothing further to say to you. I ask you to leave, now.'

She looked down her nose at Belinda, who rose and walked to the door.

'Thanks for your help, Mrs Godwin.' She paused at the door. 'Will you tell your husband when he returns from Bosham, that I'll be in contact?'

Belinda turned and walked into the farmyard.

If she'd turned back, she would have seen a look of hatred in Mrs Godwin's eyes.

On the journey to Winchester, Belinda reviewed her meeting with Mrs Godwin. It was obvious something happened in the last week that had disenchanted Mrs Godwin. There did not appear to be anyone else at the commune. Was the whole religious community revealed as a scam? Or had Mrs Godwin walked in on one of the orgies held in the barn?

And what was she doing in the barn today? There had been no sign of Saul or indeed any of the monks.

Now that Belinda thought about it, even the farm animals were missing. The whole place had an air of abandonment about it.

Had the commune broken up?

Belinda parked her car near Sir Gerald's house, this time ensuring that she had parked legally. She by passed Kingsgate Park and stepped up to Sir Gerald's front door. After several minutes of knocking she was about to admit defeat and leave, when the door swung open. A small figure, wrapped in a soiled floral pinafore, stood blinking in the late afternoon light. In a voice that reeked of the bells of St Mary-le-Bow, the woman said, 'Sorry, dear, I was up on the top floor and what with me legs being bad these days, it takes me all me time to get down 'ere. 'Ave you been waiting long?'

'Not long,' lied Belinda. 'I was hoping to find Sir Gerald at home. Is he in?'

The woman shook her head. 'Not yet. 'E's been away this last week, but I'm expecting 'im back this afternoon. I've just come in to give the place a going over before 'e arrives, but the 'ouse seems to get bigger each time I clean it.' A note of injustice had crept into her voice.

'I've come rather a long way to see him and it is important. Do you think I could wait for him?'

The cleaning woman looked her up and down, decided that Belinda looked trustworthy and swung the door wider. 'I 'spect you can, dear. As I say, Sir Gerald's due back some time this afternoon so you may have a bit of a wait, but you're welcome to do so.' She led the way into the living room where Belinda had had her previous meeting. A recently lit fire was burning in the grate. 'You can make yourself comfortable 'ere, dear. Don't expect a cuppa though, 'cos I'm way behind in me work.'

Belinda warmed her hands over the fire. 'Don't worry about me, thank you. I'll just stay by the fire until he comes.'

The woman nodded and, wiping her hands on her pinafore, made for the door. 'I've finished with the upstairs now, so I'll be down the back in the kitchen if you want me. 'Ope you don't 'ave too long to wait. You know, men ain't the most reliable creatures.'

With this insightful philosophy born of sixty or so summers – not to mention three deceased husbands – she vanished into the hall. Belinda smiled as she heard the char muttering to herself on the way to the kitchen.

Alone in the room, she was aware of an ominous silence. She glanced up at the book-lined walls that deadened any encroaching sound. Despite the warmth from the fire, chill air made her shiver. It occurred to her, as she had time before Sir Gerald returned, she might take the opportunity to search the place for her tapestry.

The drawers in the desk revealed nothing of interest. They were largely filled with hand-written notes that referred to the history of Winchester Cathedral. As well, bank statements and chequebooks cluttered up the space. Belinda gave a frustrated glance around the room. The tapestry could be anywhere; always assuming it was still in the house. On the other hand, Sir Gerald could have it with him, wherever he was.

She opened the door and stepped out into the silent hall. Opposite was what appeared to be a small dining room; next to that, a barren lounge that was obviously used as a television room. Apart from the TV set, two large chairs and a divan, there was nothing.

To her right was a staircase leading upstairs.

Belinda tiptoed to the foot of the stairs. From a door behind them, she could hear the cleaning woman singing a song made popular during the London blitz. With cat-like steps Belinda slowly mounted the stairs.

Her shoulder bag bumped against her side. She wished that she'd left it in the car but decided, as it contained her mobile telephone, and they were the most popular item stolen from cars, it was just as well that she hadn't. She held the bag firmly to stop it swinging loose. Her mouth went dry. She felt like an intruder entering unknown, and possibly dangerous, territory.

The train from London pulled into the station. Sir Gerald alighted onto the Winchester platform. Making his way with the other returning passengers, he stepped out into the damp, late afternoon air. It always pleased him to return to Winchester no matter where his travels had taken him. This time they had taken him on a most illuminating journey. As he strode off in the direction of his house, he not only felt happy at the thought of his comfortable abode which awaited him, but smiled inwardly at the cryptic secret that he had at last uncovered.

A secret that had eluded him for so many years.

At the top of the stairs, Belinda paused to catch her breath. The cleaning lady might reappear unexpectedly, while Sir Gerald himself was due any moment, so there was little time to waste. Three doors faced her. One, which was ajar, proclaimed itself to be the bathroom. That left the others to be explored. The first room proved to be Sir Gerald's bedroom. It was spartan to the point of being sterile, with only a single bed and chair, in addition to a large wardrobe. On the bed were well-worn paperback editions of Tennyson's *Idylls of the King*, and Malory's *Morte d'Arthur*. Both books were heavily annotated in spidery lace-like writing. Any decoration had been shunned, with bare walls offering no guide to the inhabitant's personality. The wardrobe revealed little other than neat rows of conventionally tailored clothing. The shelves were amply stocked with quality underwear, arranged beside linen handkerchiefs inscribed with a flamboyant "G". There was no point in Belinda searching this room, for clearly what you saw was what you got.

Stepping across the landing to the third door, she paused to listen for any new activity downstairs.

''ave you any dirty washing, Mother dear?' The misshapen arietta floated up to her as the cleaning woman continued her vocal bag of tricks.

Gently turning the doorknob, Belinda peered into the room. The blinds were drawn, so the fading winter light fought unsuccessfully to penetrate the chamber. Positioned on a desk was a computer surrounded by copious piles of documents. This seemed more fertile territory. Belinda slipped in quietly, closing the door behind her. Groping her way to the desk she switched on the table-lamp. A circle of light illuminated the documents, a print out from the computer, and a floppy disc.

Belinda picked up the nearest page and read: "I have strong reasons for believing that the Tapestry was designed in England; the probable designer was a monk familiar with the monasteries of Canterbury. It is no surprise to me that components of the story told in the Tapestry continue to thwart the viewer. To understand the Tapestry satisfactorily, it would be wise for the student to compare the work with mediaeval illustrations."

These were obviously Sir Gerald's notes. Belinda dropped the paper and looked at the blank computer screen. It was likely that all of his notes were contained on the computer disc. She switched the machine on and inserted the floppy disc. Various messages flashed on the screen and finally an instruction to log in the code phrase to open the file.

What name would he use? The logical one was "Gerald". She keyed it in.

The screen flashed the message "incorrect code".

Belinda typed in T-A-Y-L-O-R. Again she was disappointed. The computer was guarding its secrets.

Belinda began to feel apprehensive. Time was running out. Sir Gerald was due any minute. There could be a million code names to choose from.

A startling cloudburst discharged itself over Winchester. A clap of thunder shook the city. Sir Gerald took refuge in a shop doorway in Jewry Street. The residents scurried to and fro, glossy black umbrellas springing up like so many gargantuan mushrooms. Streams of water overflowed from inadequate pipes and formed tributaries that snaked across footpaths, to join the rapids cascading down the gutters. Pulling his coat close around him, Sir Gerald sniffed a sullen rebuke at the storm. Droplets of water trickled down his neck. He moved further back.

A youth with torn jeans and a dark leather jacket rushed for cover in the doorway opposite. The streetlight, feeble in the torrential deluge, provided no more than a vague impression of the young man. He shook himself like an animal, sending a spray of droplets out to meet the more formidable downpour. He ran his hand over his shorn head.

Sir Gerald gave a surprised gasp and stepped back further into the shade. He fixed his eye on the shadowy figure on the opposite pavement.

'What is he doing here?' He had spoken aloud but the roar of the rain covered his voice. He kept his eyes securely on the young man. Various thoughts ran through his brain. He hadn't expected to see him here, in Winchester. He must avoid a confrontation with the boy at all costs.

Was he being followed?

How was he to escape the youngster?

He found that he was holding his breath and felt faint with apprehension. If he could only see the boy's face.

As though in answer to his wish, the youth moved forward to scan the street. A flash of silver on his ear glittered momentarily. Sir Gerald frowned in dismay. He pressed back against the wall, so that he was totally in shadow. The movement caught the young man's eye and he looked directly across at Sir Gerald. For a moment it looked as though he was about to cross the street.

Sir Gerald prepared himself for flight. He strained his eyes through the veil of water to identify the youth.

Is it him?

The piercing clatter of approaching high heels on the pavement broke into his thoughts. A young girl, clad in a ridiculously short skirt, with a red plastic mackintosh held high above her elevated blonde coiffure, teetered unsteadily towards the youth. He slid his arm around her considerable waist. Seeking her scarlet lips, as well as cover under her red raincoat, he hastily guided the girl in the direction of the nearest pub.

As they departed, Sir Gerald saw the youth's features for the first time. He gave a tight sigh of relief. The man was a stranger.

His tense muscles relaxed and he stepped out into the street. The rain eased as suddenly as it had begun and he resumed his journey home with a lighter step.

Approaching Winchester College he slipped his hand into his pocket and removed a key ring. With chill fingers he selected his front door key.

Belinda had exhausted her imagination in searching for the code name that would give her access to the information. In a fit of frustration she hit the desk. This dislodged a document file. It fell to the floor spilling out copious amounts of paper.

Belinda hurriedly bent to gather up the documents. As fast as she picked up one sheet, another dropped to the floor.

She heard the cleaning woman enter the hall.

At that moment the mobile telephone in her shoulder bag gave a sharp ring. Belinda's heart missed a beat. She fumbled in her bag to switch it off. Her fingers seemed to be thumbs as she pressed whatever buttons they came in contact with. The ringing ceased.

Belinda held her breath. Had the woman heard? Creeping to the banister, Belinda looked over. The woman, dressed in her heavy-duty overcoat and a scarf tied over her head, emerged from the living room. She was pulling on her gloves with indignant tugs and grumbling under her breath.

Belinda caught the drift of her indignation. 'These young 'uns of t'day. Too impatient by 'arf.'

The woman clearly thought Belinda had grown tired of waiting and left the house.

The telephone in the living room rang and the woman hesitated for a moment. It was well past her going-home time; besides, tonight was her night at bingo. Unwillingly she returned to answer it, already muttering fresh grievances.

Belinda slunk back into the room. There was a certain stimulation in being an intruder in a strange house. She collected the last of the papers from the floor.

Belinda would have to wait until the woman had departed. She could hardly reappear downstairs and she would be hard pressed to explain her presence in the upstairs rooms.

As she placed the last page in the file her eye caught a list of strange words, which made little sense.

Turold

Aelfgyva

Wadard

Vital

The last word was highlighted in yellow fluorescent ink.

On instinct, and as a last-ditch effort, Belinda typed the name into the computer.

V-I-T-A-L

The screen flickered into activity and offered her the menu. Belinda sighed with satisfaction and excitement. At last she had broken the code. She scanned the menu. A collection of the contents lay before her.

Narrative.

Illumination.

Canterbury.

Winchester.

Anglo-Saxon.

Normandy.

Odo.

William.

Harold.

Fabric.

Bosham.

Godwin.

Faced with this considerable choice, Belinda chose Bosham, clicked on the file name and entered it. The screen flickered, as the computer located the file. Downstairs, the unsympathetic voice of the cleaning woman could be heard explaining to the caller for at least the fifth time, that Sir Gerald was still away, but she could take a message.

The screen cleared and Belinda began to read.

"Bosham is clearly the logical choice. Everything points to it, plus now, with the confirmation of the final section, the ambiguous imagery in the borders both top and bottom only support that confirmation."

Belinda could read no further. She heard the woman put down the telephone. Pushing the quit key, she swiftly ejected the floppy disc. With a deft movement she dropped it into her pocket. Her plan was to wait until the woman departed. Then she could sneak downstairs and escape the house before Sir Gerald arrived. Now that she had the computer disc she could study it in detail later. She reached over to the lamp switch.

Sir Gerald crossed the road near the park. He hoped the cleaning woman had lit the fire. The building would be cold after being empty for the week. He glanced up at his house and saw a light in the top room where his computer was stored. He grimaced sourly. The damned woman had not completed her work. And what was she doing in that room? He had told her a thousand times never to clean in there. He wanted no one to have even the remotest chance of seeing his files.

Even as he had these thoughts he was startled to see his front door open and the cleaning woman emerge. She slammed the door shut and scurried away in the opposite direction. He glanced up at the top window. As he did, the light was extinguished.

There was someone in his house.

As Belinda switched off the lamp, the click heightened the silence in the house. The faint gurgle of rainwater trickling through the downpipes was the only noise to break the stillness. Feeling her way in the dark, Belinda edged slowly towards the top of the stairs. She had taken only two tentative steps down, when her blood froze.

The front door was slowly opening.

A dark figure slipped, ghostlike, into the hall. By the meagre streetlight, Belinda could just discern the white hair and slim figure of Sir Gerald. He swung the door to and the imperceptible click of the lock told Belinda that she was trapped.

In the infinite darkness Belinda was fixed motionless. She felt that her very breath would give her away; reveal to Sir Gerald her presence; her illicit presence in his house. Various thoughts ran through her mind. Should she confront him with the knowledge that she knew he had retained the tapestry?

How would he react to that information? If he had lied to her, then his need for it must be very great. He might use violence to retain it. Although he was an elderly man, he was still physically fit and capable of overpowering her.

And how could she explain her presence in the darkened house? Certainly he could charge her with trespass. Even more, if he discovered the disc in her pocket.

But how to escape? Sir Gerald barred the only exit available to her.

Her eyes wide open to catch every available sliver of light, she saw Sir Gerald's dark shadowy figure move gently towards the living room door. He clearly suspected that there was an intruder concealed in the house. He gently pushed the living room door open with his fingertip. The faint ruddy glow of the fire tinged his profile.

As he was diverted with this action, with his back towards Belinda, she softly took two steps backwards. Feeling her way experimentally with each foot, she moved upwards, returning to the landing.

Looking around, she considered which room would afford her the most security. The answer was clear. None would. The only entrance and exit to the landing was via the staircase – and Sir Gerald had access to that. The rooms each had a window, but they led to nothing more than a long drop to the garden below. Belinda could not see herself surviving such a jump. Besides, the noise in opening a window would certainly attract attention.

There was no doubt about it. She was trapped.

From her high vantage point she saw Sir Gerald move towards the foot of the stairs. He glanced upwards.

Belinda snapped her head clear of his vision. The crack emanating from her rigid neck sounded loudly in her ears. Surely Sir Gerald must have heard it.

He placed one foot on the bottom stair.

Belinda took a step backwards. Her foot gently touched the door of the study. It gave a slight sigh as it swung ajar.

Sir Gerald paused on the second step. His eyes searched the darkness on the landing above him.

With her heart in her mouth, Belinda slipped silently into the study.

She heard the delicate creak of the staircase as Sir Gerald ascended. Through the crack in the door, she saw him reach the landing. He paused on the top stair, his head turning from door to door, searching for the intruder. The bathroom door stood wide open revealing its innocent interior. So too the bedroom. Belinda cursed herself for not having closed it after leaving. It would have provided a momentary diversion, if Sir Gerald had decided to search it.

Now, he swung his vision onto the half-open study door.

Within the den, Belinda, frozen with fright, pulled her coat and shoulder bag towards her, as if they possessed some magical powers that could render her invisible or at least protect her from the man's hostility.

If only she had some weapon to defend herself with.

Her hands reached out to search for such a weapon. But there was nothing within her grasp.

As he took another step towards the study, the velvety sound of Sir Gerald's shoe on the landing carpet reached her ears. Her probing fingers came in contact with something solid. The mobile phone projected from her shoulder bag. At last, a weapon. She could at least strike at Sir Gerald and hopefully make a run for it. She withdrew it and held it above her shoulder.

As she did so another thought struck her. It was a reckless and risky idea, but it might be her salvation.

She lowered the phone. With breathless anxiety, she sought to push the memory button, the speed-dial that would automatically dial Sir Gerald's telephone number. If she could lure him downstairs to answer the phone she might be able to escape.

But what was the number? What button should she press?

A speechless curse escaped her lips as she pushed at the first button her fingers came in contact with. The mobile phone gave a tiny beep. It sounded monstrous in the tense silence of the house. Had Sir Gerald heard it?

The telephone in the living room below remained mute.

Sir Gerald's faint shadow slid sleekly onto the doorjamb.

Belinda held the phone in the folds of her coat, hoping that her body would absorb the revealing beep. Her fingers plunged downwards in a last minute attempt. They made contact with another button and ground the tiny disc into the device. There was a heart stopping moment – then she heard the gratifying ring of the downstairs phone.

Sir Gerald paused at the door.

Only the wooden panel separated them.

For one moment Belinda thought he would ignore the sound and continue his search.

She had stopped breathing. Then, the welcome soft rustle of Sir Gerald's clothing, as he turned and edged his way in the dark, back down the staircase.

Belinda gulped in a lungful of fresh air. She stole onto the landing. She feared her weak legs would fail her. The urgent ringing of the phone filled the shadowy house.

A beam of pale light spilled across the hallway. She heard Sir Gerald pick up the telephone. Belinda took a tentative step down the staircase, her heart beating in her ribs.

'4695,' Sir Gerald gave his telephone number, his voice rigid with tension.

The great danger was that he would hang up the minute he realised that there was no caller on the other end of the phone. Belinda had only a few seconds to reach the door.

Hesitantly, she moved downwards.

'Hello? Hello, damn you.' Sir Gerald sounded angry and confused. Belinda hoped his loud voice would mask any noise she might make. 'Is anyone there?' By now his voice was full of rage. Belinda took a deep breath. She plunged forward into the hall, her feet barely skimming over the carpet-covered stairs. In a few steps she had crossed the hall. As she passed the living room door, she glimpsed Sir Gerald and heard the loud crash as he slammed the telephone down.

Her fingers closed over the door handle as she pulled it towards her.

It remained shut. Unyielding.

Terror now cloaking her shoulders, she glanced back. Sir Gerald's shadow lengthened across the hall carpet as he approached the living room door.

The lock to the front door was like cruel ice in her fingers. She turned it. The lock's mechanism engaged. It clicked noisily. With all her strength, Belinda wrenched the heavy door open. She flung herself out into the bitter night, into the embracing blackness and, half falling down the rain sodden steps, reached the security of the street.

Each breath was a stab of pain. She ran helter-skelter into the pitch-black. Glancing over her shoulder, she saw the murky silhouette of Sir Gerald as he stood at his front door, the warm yellow light of the hall lamp spilling out into the wintry street.

Safe for the moment, Belinda was engulfed by a new anxiety. Had Sir Gerald seen her? And did he recognise her?

Eleven

The moment she returned from Winchester, Belinda drove straight to Mark's house. He was roused from a half-slumber in front of the television screen, which was telecasting a less than glorious one-day cricket match from Melbourne between England and Australia. Quickly she related the events of the past few hours.

'And this is the disc from his computer.' She flourished her trophy.

Mark, stunned by the torrent of words, now gave her an incredulous look. 'You stole it?'

'Well ... more like borrowed,' replied a defensive Belinda, 'but if he stole my tapestry, then we're even,' she concluded righteously.

Before Mark could continue his censorious remarks, she turned and went to his study. Mark followed, pausing briefly to watch the dismissal of the English captain for an embarrassingly low score.

He watched as Belinda switched on the computer and inserted the disc. 'Well, I've got some news for you too. I checked with my father's old chums in Whitehall. It seems that the Godwins moved back to England about six months ago. Prior to that they'd been managing an hotel on the continent.'

Belinda's attention was on the computer. 'Oh?' she replied half-heartedly.

'You may show a little more interest, when you hear where the hotel was.'

'Where was that?' asked Belinda, with no more enthusiasm than she had shown previously.

'A little town called St Laurent on the Normandy coast.'

'Uh-huh,' Belinda said absently.

'A town that's only eighteen kilometres from Bayeux.'

Belinda swung around to face Mark. 'That's where the Tapestry's held.'

Mark nodded knowingly, a boastful smile on his face. 'You're not the only one who can do detective work.' He stepped forward and sat beside Belinda. 'Now, what's on this disc that you thought was so important?'

'All sorts of things about the Bayeux Tapestry. Canterbury, King William, Harold and Bosham. That's what attracted my attention, because we had just been there.'

The computer screen sprang into life and unfolded the menu.

Mark sat beside her. 'Where should we start?'

'Everything seems to centre around Harold, so let's begin with him.'

Belinda keyed in Harold's name. The menu for Harold replaced the previous screen.

'Go to his death,' muttered Mark, finding himself drawn into the thrill of the search. The facts of Harold's death unfolded on the screen and they read it through in silence.

'Well, that doesn't tell us anything we didn't know,' said Mark in a disappointed voice. 'We already assume he died either by being shot in the eye by an arrow or when his thigh was slashed open.'

'But it tells us where he was buried,' replied Belinda excitedly, 'at Waltham Abbey. Where's that?'

'Somewhere north of London.'

'Then let's go there. We have Sir Gerald's guide to everything relating to the Tapestry. If we follow it we may solve the mystery.' She leapt to her feet. 'Bring your laptop. We can go from clue to clue.'

Mark switched off the computer. 'Why not? It's as silly an idea as you've ever had,' he said, with a note of disdain.

'What's that supposed to mean?' asked Belinda, her voice tinged with resentment.

'You expect me to just drop everything and go gallivanting all over the country? I do have a job to go to.'

'Rubbish,' snapped Belinda, 'you said yourself, only the other day, that it was impossible to sell property at Christmas time, so you can surely take some time off.'

'Maybe, but hadn't you better look after Hazel's shop? It's the best time of year for her, what with people wanting Christmas gifts.' Belinda was chastened. Mark was right, but she would not admit it.

'Look, the shop has hardly been open at all recently. Another day won't do any harm.' She hoped she sounded convincing. Apparently she did, for Mark gave a sigh of acquiescence.

'OK. But at least let's wait until daylight.'

"HAROLD KING OF ENGLAND OBIIT 1066."

The carved inscription on the memorial stone was difficult to read in the fast fading afternoon light. Easier to read, was the legend on the flat slab before it.

"THIS STONE MARKS THE POSITION OF THE HIGH ALTAR BEHIND WHICH KING HAROLD IS SAID TO HAVE BEEN BURIED IN 1066."

Belinda and Mark, surrounded by the ruins of Waltham Abbey, stood before the stones. As they turned away and walked disconsolately back to Mark's car, Belinda felt a wave of disappointment. 'I really thought we'd find a clue here, Mark. But it's just a ruin.'

'We're not even sure if it is Harold's burial place,' Mark said, tightening his scarf against the evening damp. 'William wanted to dump his enemy's body in the sea, so that there would be no possibility of Harold being considered a martyr and his tomb a centre for rebellious groups.'

'Now you tell me!'

'I've been doing some research. Things changed when

Harold's mistress, Edith Swan Neck, identified his body on the battlefield and appealed to William to have him buried here. Or so the story goes.'

'Do you think she had a long neck? Edith, I mean. Swan Neck?'

'That's a typical female question. Nothing to do with the matter at hand.'

Belinda gave him a disparaging look. 'I just wondered, that's all. It's such a funny name.'

Mark continued, 'Besides, how exactly does Harold tie in with your missing tapestry?'

Belinda frowned. 'I'm not sure how any of it fits together, but somehow it must. William, Sir Gerald, Bosham, the Godwins, Odo and Harold.'

'Harold, the unlucky,' muttered Mark.

'What did you say?'

'I've just remembered. Something we were taught at school. The original inscription on the grave read, "Harold, the unlucky". This was the last abbey to be disbanded when Henry the Eighth dissolved the monasteries. Being here brought it all back. Funny the things you remember.'

Belinda shrugged. 'Well, we're out of luck too. At least here. Let's go home.'

Mark shivered and pulled his jacket about him. He looked up at the threatening sky. 'It's getting late and I wouldn't be surprised if it snowed. I don't feel like driving back to Bath tonight. Let's stay in London and we can get an early start tomorrow on our next clue.'

Mrs Godwin sat at the heavily scrubbed kitchen table. The farmhouse was silent and cold. She was alone now in the deserted community, and the silence was getting on her nerves. What sound did penetrate the solid stone walls, was muted by a light fall of snow. As she poured her third glass of whisky she recalled her childhood, the anticipation of Santa Claus's arrival, the pantomimes and her longing for a 'White Christmas'. Now she only sought warmth, and mouthed a silent profanity against the blanket of snow covering the countryside.

On the table before her was a bizarre jigsaw puzzle she was creating, rather than solving. The colourful pieces lay scattered over the tabletop, some spilling down onto the kitchen floor. She shivered from the cold, as much as from the whisky, as its compassionate warmth flowed through her. The large dressmaker's scissors she held weighed her hand down as she reached for the final piece of her puzzle. She drew it towards her.

It was the photograph from the Bayeux Tapestry of King Harold's slaughter. Many times she had seen it displayed in the chapel, many times she had been stimulated by it. Now she felt nothing but revulsion. The heavy photographic paper yielded reluctantly to the sharp blade of the scissors, but her determined fingers, sore and pinched from her efforts, forced the blades closed. Filled with determination, she cut the photograph into strips.

As she released them, the scissors clattered onto the stone floor. Pausing only for a moment to massage her bruised fingers, she began to tear the strips into shreds. She worked steadfastly, until all that remained was a pile of coloured scraps. They joined the other fragments. Pausing a moment for breath, she gathered as much as she could hold, carried them to the fire and handful by handful, heaped the debris onto the hot coals. The fire, welcoming the nourishment, blazed enthusiastically. Mrs Godwin stood, her hands raised onto the mantelpiece, staring down into the feverish eruption. Her eyes gleamed with reflected light, while a satisfied smile curved her lips. Standing aggressively over the fire, she fed the flames, until all sign of the photographs had vanished; until the heat receded and all that remained was the shimmering coals, with an occasional blue flame dancing wraith-like over the surface.

Only then did she sigh and relax. She dropped to her seat at the table and drained the whisky glass of its contents.

A distant clock chimed the hour of nine. Mrs Godwin looked out of the window into the dark night. Reluctantly she rose. Taking a knife from a drawer, she sliced some bread from a large loaf and placed some cheese between the slices. Icy water from the kitchen tap flowed into a plastic cup. Then taking a large electric torch, she gathered up the rough-hewn sandwich and water and stepped out into the darkness.

The beam from the torch cut a swathe through the falling snow. It fell in regimented vertical lines through the still air.

Crossing the yard, she came to the barn, opened the door and entered. The yard, now deprived of the torchlight, reverted to the ghostly grey of the tumbling snow.

Inside the barn, Mrs Godwin stepped tentatively over the straw covered floor. She found her way to the foot of worn wooden steps and flinched with nervousness in the dark, evil smelling surrounds. Cautiously she made her way up, the torchlight creating accompanying phantoms on the grimy walls.

Before her, on the landing, was a door with a hefty padlock. She fumbled with the key, juggling the food, water and torch. The lock fell free and she pushed the door open. Holding the torch before her, so that the ray of light illuminated a small room, she stepped forward.

As her eyes grew familiar with the half-light, she saw amid mounting alarm, that the room was empty.

At the same time she acknowledged this, a black apparition flew through the air and struck her down.

Mrs Godwin fell as though lifeless onto the squalid floor.

'Vital, Turgold, Aelfgyva and Wadard.'

The words flickered onto the notebook computer screen. Seated in a secluded corner of the London hotel, Belinda and

Mark, refreshed by a satisfying dinner, had taken their coffee in the lounge and set the notebook up on the coffee table. There were few guests to disturb them, so they were able to peruse the information contained on Sir Gerald's disc with ease.

'They're the words I saw on the piece of paper in Sir Gerald's study.'

'Let's see what they mean,' said Mark, as he scrolled down the screen.

'They're the names of associates of Odo, William the Conqueror's half-brother,' Belinda read aloud, pointing to the information as it was divulged. 'Odo was the Earl of Kent and Vital and Wadard managed lands for him there. Probably they were his henchmen.'

'Henchmen? What a quaint expression,' said Mark, with a smile.

'Well, you know what I mean. If Odo was like a mediaeval Godfather …'

'Godfather? Do you think he stuffed cotton wool in his cheeks and sounded like Marlon Brando?'

'Idiot,' replied Belinda tartly. 'All I mean is that they were probably in Odo's pay and did his dirty work.'

'But that doesn't explain why Sir Gerald would use one of the henchmen's names as his code word to gain access to the files.'

Belinda shrugged. 'Who knows why? Perhaps he thought it obscure enough for no one to decipher.' Further information spilled onto the screen. 'And look,' she cried excitedly, 'their names appear on the Bayeux Tapestry. I wonder why?'

'Here's the reason.' Mark gulped down his coffee and gestured at the screen. 'See. A man named as Vital informed William that King Harold's army had been sighted, before the Battle of Hastings.'

'So, he was an important man not only to William but to Odo as well? Do you think he was a double agent?'

Mark sank back into the leather-covered chair. 'I had no idea you had such a command of underworld expressions. Henchmen. Double agents. But it's peculiar how we keep coming back to Odo. He was William's half-brother and, as the Earl of Kent, held most of the land around Canterbury, which meant he probably had a lot of power.'

'And Canterbury distrusted Odo, or at least the church hierarchy did, because they thought he wanted their wealth,' said Belinda thoughtfully. 'I remember now, the Vicar told me that Odo was accused of stealing the treasures held by the abbeys and churches in Kent. In fact, I believe the Archbishop of Canterbury took him to court.' She glanced across at Mark. 'Should we go to Canterbury tomorrow?'

'I can't see what good it can do. It would be like Waltham Abbey. Just a collection of inarticulate stones. We need to do some serious thinking. I believe we've most of the clues. It's just a matter of piecing them together into some semblance of order.' He stood up. 'Besides, there's something you seem to have forgotten.'

Belinda snapped the laptop shut and rose. 'What's that?'

'What's happened to Hazel?'

A flush of guilt overcame Belinda. She realised that she had indeed temporally forgotten her friend. 'You're right,' she remarked guiltily.

'I think we'd better head home first thing in the morning. If there's still no sign of her, we must check with the police.' Belinda nodded her silent agreement. They began to walk towards the lifts. Suddenly, Belinda grasped Mark's arm.

'Look,' she whispered urgently, and nodded towards the hotel foyer.

Making his way across the lobby was Charles Godwin. He paused midway and appeared to be uncertain as to which way to go. He glanced in the direction where Mark and Belinda were standing. For a moment he appeared stunned at their presence.

'Mark, don't let him get away!'

As though he'd heard, Godwin sprang into action. He turned

towards the front door of the hotel and rushed across the foyer. Startled guests cleared a path for him as he disappeared into the street. With a cry, Mark immediately gave chase, further alarming the already shocked patrons. They turned their censorious gaze on Belinda. Such violent activity was not condoned in London, W1. Belinda, with as much savoir faire as she could muster, crossed the foyer and emerged into the street. She was in time to see Mark sprinting around the corner.

Godwin had a head start. He was heading towards Cavendish Square.

Mark, his adrenaline flowing, ran swiftly after him, drawing closer by the minute.

The two racing figures attracted the attention of the crowds sight-seeing the Christmas lights. Some cheered them on as if witnessing an exuberant Yuletide fling. Others, more faultfinding, frowned and escorted their partners in other directions.

Godwin, pausing for breath, glanced over his shoulder. Mark was bearing down on him. He sped off and turned into Regent Street.

As Mark followed he ran into a wall of Londoners, all agog with the spectacle of the glittering Christmas decorations. In the distance he saw Godwin swallowed up by the crowd at Oxford Circus. He slowed to a walk and, fighting for his breath, realised that he had lost the chase.

Mark, loudly and belligerently, gave vent to an expletive, which takes its mediaeval origins from the Middle Dutch work, Fokken.

Only then did he realise that he was standing in the middle of a busload of country schoolchildren, most of whom, by their giggles, indicated that they were familiar with the vulgar word and its various applications.

Not so their austere and decorous female teachers who regarded his indiscretion with scandalised expressions and confirmed their opinion of the male sex.

'The Borders of the Bayeux Tapestry serve not only as a framework but are an indispensable detail in the story conveyed,' Belinda read aloud from the notebook screen. She and Mark were driving back to Bath and while Mark's attention was on the road, Belinda, laptop balanced on her knees, was browsing through Sir Gerald's commentary on the Tapestry. She had reread its history, confirmed the belief that Odo had commissioned the work and that it was probably made under the mastery of the monks at Canterbury. She had just finished reading aloud to Mark, comments on the significance of symbolic animals within the borders and their connection with the basic narrative.

'That rings a bell,' she said thoughtfully.

'What does?' asked Mark, as he turned off the A4 onto the road to Milford.

'The remarks about the border on the Tapestry. I remember Sir Gerald going on about that when I first called on him.' She stared out into the passing countryside as she sought to recall his observations. 'Something about the borders being more than just pretty ornamental frames. He said they had a bearing on the main part of the Tapestry.'

'Like an addendum?'

Belinda gave him a mocking smile. 'My, my. Such big words.' Mark gave her an amused sidelong glance. 'But sorry to disappoint you,' Belinda continued. 'Although that's what Sir Gerald called it, he clearly thought they meant something else. Something more integral, I fancy. It had to do with what he called the Winchester style.'

'Meaning what, exactly?'

Belinda waved her hand in a gesture of frustration. 'I'm not sure, but it seems that in mediaeval times, the monks at Winchester developed a style that incorporated the borders into the general story.'

'I imagine you mean when they made their illuminated religious books?' queried Mark.

'Do I? Yes, I suppose I do. Anyway, apparently the border was not just a frame and that technique was characteristic of Winchester. It seems that style was adapted by whoever made the Tapestry. Which is why it was thought to have been made in Winchester, although now Canterbury is the hot favourite.'

'Is that important to us?'

'Well, I was wondering. If it meant something in the Bayeux Tapestry, might it not likewise mean something in mine?'

'What was shown in the borders in yours?'

Belinda gave a shrug. 'Not much that I can recall. Some church paraphernalia. A cross. A chalice. Things like that.

'But wasn't there a burial?' asked Mark, as he slowed at a set of crossroads.

'Yes. It showed a monk being buried. And the remains of a skeleton.'

'How do you think they relate to the main needlework?'

'I can't see how they would. That showed William the Conqueror being crowned king.'

'But not in Westminster Abbey.'

Belinda nodded thoughtfully. 'Well, we all agree, it looks like the church at Bosham.' She was silent for a moment. 'But if my border does have a bearing on that, what does it mean?'

'That I can't tell you. But what I can tell you is both Sir Gerald and Godwin want the tapestry. Godwin because he's mad enough to think he's the King of England and Sir Gerald – well, who knows what he wants it for.'

'If the Godwins lived near Bayeux they could have seen the real thing every day. His wife said he was obsessed with it and believed there was a missing panel. The one I found at Kidbrooke House, do you think?'

'But didn't Sir Gerald say it couldn't have been a part of the original Tapestry?'

'He did. But can we believe that? What if it was the real thing? It would be worth millions.'

'Priceless,' muttered Mark. 'Which means you could never sell it. It probably belongs to the Crown anyway.'

'Wouldn't the French want it? To put with the rest of it?'

'Like the Greeks and the Elgin Marbles? Probably. But I wouldn't like their chances. If it is part of the original Tapestry, you can bet the government would hang onto it whatever the cost.'

'So what value is it to Sir Gerald?'

'There are some collectors who pay vast sums for treasures just to lock them away from the public. They seem to get a kinky thrill out of possessing something of great value that only they can see or hold.'

'Well, that could explain Sir Gerald's eagerness to get his hands on it. But what about Godwin?'

'Probably the same reason.'

'No. There's more to it than that. Suppose he saw it on display at Kidbrooke House. If he was obsessed with his claim to the crown, he may have wanted to destroy it.'

'Because it showed William being crowned you mean?' Mark shook his head. 'No. The whole world knows William was king. What would destroying your tapestry prove?'

'I see what you mean, but what did Mrs Godwin imply when she said her husband was eager to dig it up? Dig what up? She said he was still at Bosham. What was he doing there? Why was his farm deserted and what was he doing in London last night?'

'Questions, questions, questions. If we knew the answers,' replied Mark, 'there would be no mystery.'

Mark pulled over to the side of the road and Belinda was surprised to find herself at her own front gate.

'But for a start, I suggest we examine that colour photograph you have,' Mark continued, as he climbed out of the car. 'Perhaps if we study the borders again we can make some sense out of it, if we really try.'

They walked through the garden to the front door. 'Before I do anything else,' said Belinda slipping the key into the lock and entering the hall, 'I must ring Hazel and see if she's come home. If not, we'd better advise the police.'

She walked to the rear of the house and stepped into the long room. A roaring fire was blazing in the fireplace and a woman was seated nearby, her head encircled by a bloody bandage.

Belinda gave a cry of surprise.

For the woman who turned to look at her was Mrs Godwin.

Twelve

The two women looked at each other. Belinda in astonishment, Mrs Godwin in dazed apprehension. The chink-chink of ice in a glass filled the tense silence and preceded a familiar, penetrating, voice. 'I suppose a formal introduction at this late stage would be considered anachronistic.' Hazel stood in the doorway, the omnipresent gin in her hand.

A tableau of three quick-tempered women confronted Mark as he entered the room. His masculine insight warned him that this setting had all the volatility of a war zone.

Belinda's eyes widened as she watched Hazel stride across the room. She opened her mouth to speak, but the older woman insisted on having the first word.

'A fine friend *you* turned out to be!' The accusation was hurled at Belinda. 'Have you any idea of what I've been through? Kidnapped. Locked up. And where were you while all this was happening?'

Belinda's mouth remained open, firstly from the sudden appearance of her friend, and secondly from the fierce accusations being flung at her.

'I've always said, if you want something done you should do it yourself,' continued Hazel, warming to the theme. 'Don't expect others to come to your aid. I could have been murdered!' she declared with a theatrical shudder.

'Oh, shut up, you stupid cow.'

It was Hazel's turn to stare open mouthed. Mrs Godwin snapped the caustic remark at her and turned to face Belinda. 'She was never in any real danger, at least, not from me.'

Mark, not wishing to be witness to a catfight, took control.

'Would someone just explain what's going on?'

Belinda regained her speech. 'Mark, this is Mrs Godwin. You remember? She and her husband have the religious community in Norton St Philip.'

Mark nodded acknowledgement to the woman. She ignored him and fingered her bandaged brow.

'Hazel, instead of making wild statements,' he demanded, 'perhaps you'd tell us where you've been for the past few days and why Mrs Godwin is here.' He seated himself in a chair. Stretching his legs before him, he settled in for what he suspected would be a tortuous route to the truth.

Hazel gestured at Mrs Godwin, spilling a quantity of her gin in the process. 'You'd better ask her,' she snarled. Belinda and Mark turned their attention to the woman seated on the sofa.

'The truth is, my husband is a bastard,' began Mrs Godwin vehemently.

Mark raised a restraining hand. 'Marital confessions are not relevant just at this moment, Mrs Godwin. Would you simply stick to recent events?'

'I am, in a way, because it's only in the past few days that I realised just what sort of a man my husband is.'

'And what sort of man is that?' encouraged Belinda, feeling that they would be there all day at this rate.

'Tell them what you told me,' snapped Hazel.

Mrs Godwin glanced at her and back to Belinda. 'Well, you met him. You must know how convincing he can be. I really believed in everything he told me. Everything he claimed.'

'What did he claim?' asked Mark.

'It probably sounds absurd, but he claimed that he was descended from King Harold. He'd got hold of some family papers somewhere and was convinced that he was a direct descendant. It became a passion with him. We've spent the last few years tracking down any piece of evidence that could support his claim.'

'But what about the religious community,' interrupted Belinda, 'how did that fit in with his claim?'

'I was never sure about that. He'd always been religious, and when he told me he wanted to start a community devoted to the ideals of St Augustine, I saw nothing wrong with that.'

'Why St Augustine?' demanded Mark.

'I never knew, except that St Augustine introduced Christianity to England, or at least in Kent, when he founded a church in Canterbury.'

'Ah, yes. Canterbury.' Belinda nodded with satisfaction.

'I didn't have strong religious feelings,' continued Mrs Godwin, 'but I could see no harm in what he proposed, and the life style, living on a farm after years of managing one star hotels, well, it appealed to me. It seemed a good way to live. At first. Then the infatuation with Harold and the Bayeux Tapestry became an obsession. I didn't understand it ever. Not really. He built it into the religious life at the community.'

'It didn't seem a very religious life, from what I saw,' said Belinda.

Mrs Godwin glanced at her. 'It wasn't like that at the beginning. It really was a peaceful community. Self-sufficient to a degree. A contemplative life and on the whole, fairly happy. It was when he became fixated with the Bayeux Tapestry and the depiction of Harold's death that things changed. Most of the original young members of the community drifted away. I don't suppose they saw much value in that, from a religious point of view. That's when I began to wonder what was going on. He brought these rough boys in, youths that didn't seem that religious to my way of thinking.'

'Do you mean Saul?' asked Belinda.

The woman looked at her and then averted her eyes. 'Saul was the first of the rough ones. He arrived suddenly one day. I loathed him on sight. My husband seemed to spend a lot of time with him, which seemed strange to me. After all, Godwin was an educated man and his friendship with that …' she sought the word, '… creature … was uncharacteristic. So … extraordinary. About that time he began to exclude me from his activities. He kept to himself and barely discussed the running of the household with me.' She glanced again to Belinda. 'That's why I was so off-hand with you. I suspected that he was having an affair with you. We'd been to your house, and then you turned up at the farm, claiming to be in need of religious help. By that stage I had lost my belief in the community, knew it was a sham, so naturally I suspected your motives.'

'When you came to my house,' said Belinda, 'you were more interested in the auction at Kidbrooke House?'

Mrs Godwin nodded. 'My husband had visited Kidbrooke House at some time and had seen a tapestry square there. He said it reminded him of the Bayeux Tapestry and he would have liked it.'

'Did he ever try to get it?'

'I believe he did offer to buy it from the owner but the old man wouldn't sell.'

'When was that?'

Mrs Godwin thought, running her hand over her bandaged head and frowning. 'A few weeks back, I think. He and Saul and one of the other boys were away for a couple of days. They'd gone looking for recruits for the community. Or so they said. While they were away, I discovered some papers in his desk that showed he had set out to visit Kidbrooke House with a purpose.'

'Can you be more accurate about just when that visit took place?' asked Mark.

'Is it that important?' said Mrs Godwin wearily.

'I'm afraid it is,' replied Belinda.

'Well, it was some time after he had the ceremony commemorating the death of King Harold. That was the fourteenth of October, so I suppose it would have been early November.'

Belinda and Mark exchanged a glance.

'But it was all a bit silly really, commemorating the

anniversary,' continued Mrs Godwin, 'because he never really knew if Harold was killed.'

'What did you say?' asked Belinda, suddenly alert.

Mrs Godwin shrugged. 'My husband came to believe the folk story that Harold survived the slaughter and was rescued by some peasants, who nursed him back to health. His lady friend, Edith Swan Neck, who was probably in on the act, identified the wrong body on the battlefield, allowing Harold to escape.'

'But what happened to him after that?' Belinda asked eagerly.

'There are several stories. One has him surviving in Chester. The one my husband favoured had Harold living in Canterbury, where he lived as a monk in a hermitage, secretly watching William whenever the king worshipped at the cathedral. I believe the possibility that Harold did not die gave my husband encouragement, if he could prove he was descended from one of the six or so illegitimate children Harold had with Edith.'

'Well, you did say your husband was a bastard,' growled Hazel.

Having been ignored for the past few minutes she was determined to make herself the centre of attention once more. 'You may not have noticed, but I *am* present at the moment and you have not asked me where I have been and what tortures I have suffered.'

Belinda gave her a guilty look. 'I'm sorry, Hazel. You're right. Where did you get to?'

'If you remember,' said Hazel acidly, 'you left me sitting outside the church at Bosham. You were away for an interminable age, so I went for a stroll. Suddenly I came upon her.' She gestured at Mrs Godwin. 'With her was a man I now know was her husband, and our friend from the other week, Saul. We recognised each other immediately and before I could do anything, I was bundled into a car and kidnapped.'

Mrs Godwin nodded in agreement. 'What she says is true. I was stunned. Saul held her down in the back of the car while my husband drove like a mad thing. All the way back, I pleaded for him to tell me what he was doing.

'It wasn't until we were back at the farm and Hazel was securely locked in the barn that he even spoke to me. Even then I still didn't understand what was going on. I was told that I had to keep her prisoner until he and Saul returned from the Bosham dig. If I didn't do what I was told, Saul would deal with me. I pleaded with my husband to explain his actions but he struck me. He told me to keep my mouth shut, to do what I was told and I wouldn't get hurt. I asked why he was going back to Bosham and he said, "Because that's where it is".

'I asked him what would happen to the community and he laughed and said, it had served its purpose and it, and I, could go to hell.'

Hazel, who felt that the centre of activity had again drifted away from her, advanced into the middle of the room. 'In the meantime, I was trussed up in the barn like a Christmas turkey, being fed the most appalling muck and wondering when my so-called friends would rescue me. Eventually I got free of the ropes and found a piece of wood. I bopped madam here, on the head, and brought her here as my prisoner.'

Mrs Godwin gave her a look of pity. 'I'm sorry to spoil your heroic story, Hazel, but I came of my own free will. I want Saul and my husband caught just as much as you, particularly now that I know Saul beat you up.

'I realise that Charles is involved in something crooked and that his interest in religion and the belief that he is descended from Harold, is just a cover for whatever scam he is working.'

Belinda rose and stood in front of Mrs Godwin. 'Tell me truthfully. Do you know what is so special about the church at Bosham?'

There was a moment before Mrs Godwin answered. 'No,' she replied, shaking her head. 'But I do know that whatever is there, means more to my husband than anything on earth.'

Hazel snored softly, the faint firelight softening her features. She had dozed off after dinner, and the fourth re-telling of her adventures. Mrs Godwin had returned to the farm, determined to pack. She had also resolved to leave her husband. Belinda and Mark sat side by side on the sofa, the laptop open before them, a bottle of port at their elbow and the illustrated book detailing the history of the Bayeux Tapestry beside them.

'Canterbury seems to be a re-occurring theme through all this,' said Belinda, as she sipped her port. 'We presume the Tapestry was made there. The churchmen didn't like Odo. They accused him of knocking off the Cathedral's treasures. Furthermore Godwin based his community on St Augustine of Canterbury.'

'True,' replied Mark, 'but there is also Bosham and Waltham Abbey.'

'You yourself said that Waltham Abbey provided no clues, but you're right about Bosham. What's the connection with Canterbury?' Belinda scanned the computer screen before her and read its report. '"Bosham is clearly the logical choice. Everything points to it. Now, with the confirmation of the final section, the ambiguous imagery in the borders both top and bottom only support that confirmation."'

She leant forward and opened the illustrated book. 'I'm certain that Sir Gerald was writing about my tapestry. We know the borders in the Bayeux Tapestry itself were more than decorative and should be considered part of the overall picture. The animals shown are allegorical, the appearance of Halley's Comet is a side issue to the main story, and the Normans are shown looting the dead during the Battle of Hastings.'

'So?' asked Mark as he poured himself another port. He waved the bottle at Belinda and raised inquisitive eyebrows. She shook her head and reached for the colour photograph of her tapestry square.

'In the borders of *my* tapestry there are religious objects and a dead monk being buried, probably in a graveyard, because there are the skeletons of previous corpses. I don't suppose it shows William's burial?'

'William wasn't a monk, nor was he buried at Bosham, or for that matter, in Westminster Abbey. Besides, he had grown very fat and when they attempted to stuff his jumbo-size corpse into the coffin, he burst open and stunk the church out.'

Belinda gave him an odd look.

'Before you ask, I remember that from school as well. We used to call him the royal stink bomb.' Mark grinned widely.

Aware of Belinda's unamused critical stare, he thought it prudent to return to the topic under discussion. 'But if yours is only a recent copy, the borders would be purely decorative.'

'Maybe,' replied Belinda doubtfully, 'but why show such a dramatic scene? I grant you the top border could be considered ornamental, religious objects and things, but why the burial of a monk? Surely if they were to be decorative, whoever made it would have used flowers or animals, not something so specific as a burial.'

Mark took the photograph and studied it. 'Well, let's look at what we've got. In the centre illustration we have William being crowned king.'

'In Bosham church,' concluded Belinda.

'Which is where Harold prayed before he went to Normandy. Plus, his father's buried there.'

'Let's ignore William for the moment,' said Belinda, a note of excitement creeping into her voice. 'That leaves us with the Bosham Church and the burial of a monk.'

Mark leant forward, some of Belinda's excitement reaching him. Belinda grasped the photograph. 'Right,' she continued, 'so if we follow the allusion made in the border, the burial took place at Bosham church, and we know that monk – what was his name – Diesel?'

'Dicul. A seventh century Irish monk.'

Belinda nodded in agreement. 'Right. Dicul was buried there.

That little man we met at the church, the one who played the organ, he said there was a burial chamber for monks within the crypt of the church.'

'Which means what?'

Belinda's shoulders sagged in dismay. 'You're right. It does seem pointless information.' Her brows furrowed in speculation. 'Unless … unless the information in the top border is included.'

'But how?

'We know the Tapestry was made in Canterbury. Imagine for a moment that my square is a missing part of the original. The end panel probably. Whoever made it was simply putting in a message, a hidden message to be deciphered by someone who could read the signs.'

'But what signs?'

Belinda almost jumped out of her chair with excitement. 'I think I know. The churchmen at Canterbury reluctantly acknowledged William as king. They disliked his half-brother, Odo, and accused him of stealing their treasures, treasures that would have included gold chalices and gold plates. Maybe to protect their valuable possessions, the monks buried them so that Odo could not get his hands on them.'

'Buried them where?'

Belinda pointed excitedly at the photograph. 'Read the signs. The treasure was buried with the corpse of a monk, probably in his coffin. And as Canterbury had remained loyal to Harold, why not bury it in a safe place far away from Canterbury, but in a site that had some connection with the man they still considered their king. At the church in Bosham.'

She sat back in her chair, a look of triumph on her face.

'That's what it's all about. Sir Gerald and Godwin are after buried treasure.'

Thirteen

'That'll be fifteen pounds for the night, dear. Each that is, and breakfast normally at eight, but any time really, so long as you give me plenty of notice.'

Belinda and Mark followed Mrs O'Brien's robust frame as she bustled into the bedsitting room of the B&B at Bosham. In her arms she carried a gargantuan ginger cat, which surveyed the new visitors with proprietorial eyes.

'We've been quite busy the past few weeks,' she continued, as she adjusted the central heating, 'particularly for this time of year. I expect it's the work they're doing at the church. Such comings and goings, aren't there, Mr Pudding.' This last comment was addressed to the cat cloistered in her arms. The cat did not deign to comment.

'What work is that?' asked Belinda, thinking she had never known a cat more aptly named. She sat on the bed and secretly tested its resilience.

'Oh, it's yet another dig in the church grounds.' The landlady walked to the window. 'You'd think they'd let those poor souls rest in peace, but no. They have to be forever digging away. This lot started early in the week. Funny time to do it, don't you think? The middle of winter? It's usually in the summer.'

'Have you had any of the excavation crew staying here?' asked Mark, as he surveyed the distant earthworks. He noted the safety barriers erected along the side of the church.

'I believe most of them are staying with Mrs Williams and Mrs Jackson over t'other side of the village. Done a deal, I shouldn't be surprised,' replied Mrs O'Brien, showing the cloven foot. 'There was one chap. Stayed here on and off recently. Spent a lot of time hanging around the church. I can't say I took to him personally, but in my position, I can't be too judgmental. With a B&B you have to accept all types. All the same, I didn't much care for some of his companions. Young toughs, they were. I'm glad they didn't stay here. They only came to visit my tenant.'

'Do you recall his name?' asked Belinda.

Mrs O'Brien pursed her lips and wracked her brain. 'Can't say that I do. When you have people coming and going, they all become a blur, really. But it'll be in my registration book. I'll look it up for you, if you like.'

'Don't bother. Would it have been Godwin?' Mark asked.

Mrs O'Brien looked from one to the other. 'I do believe it was. I do hope he wasn't a friend of yours, after what I said. No offence meant.'

'Don't worry, Mrs O'Brien. He's no friend, but we do know him,' smiled Belinda. 'When did he stay here?'

'On and off over the past few weeks. Last time was at the weekend. There was a woman too and that nasty boy. They appeared very interested in the church, which seemed strange to me. None of them looked the religious type.'

'Has there been anyone else? A tall grey haired, distinguished looking man?'

'I can only imagine you mean Sir Gerald,' Mrs O'Brien replied, beaming smugly. 'He's been coming to Bosham on and off for the best part of three weeks. I think he's got something to do with the dig. Lord no, dear, he only stays with Mrs Williams. Twenty-five pounds per person a night she charges. Mind you she's got four stars in the B&B guide, but then she had money to start with. Some of us didn't have her good fortune to begin with, did we dear?' she concluded tartly, thinking of the lone star her establishment merited in the guidebook and mentally questioning, once again, the manner in which her opposition acquired so posh an enterprise.

The evening was clear and chill. Belinda and Mark, having feasted on steak and kidney pie at the Anchor Bleu pub, were strolling along the foreshore, the village lights reflecting across the waters of the inlet at Chichester Harbour. Yachts moored on the passive water rocked gently and the clink of nautical trappings sounded musically in the hushed night.

'So, Sir Gerald has been visiting Bosham for some time. He must have had suspicions about the church and my tapestry confirmed his hunch,' said Belinda, pulling her scarf around her neck.

Mark nodded agreement. 'Tomorrow we'll watch the dig. If he turns up we can confront him.'

They sauntered towards the church and the sound of the choir rehearsing Christmas carols intensified as they drew near. An inadequate warning lamp on the safety barriers surrounding the dig flickered in the darkening churchyard. The smell of damp earth, mixed with the intense mustiness of long buried rock, made Belinda shiver with distaste. She remembered reading that the church was built upon the site of a Roman basilica and thought it unfortunate that the ancient stones were once more being exposed to human interference.

The travel alarm clock showed 2:00 a.m. in ghostly fluorescent green as Belinda sat up in bed. She pulled her dressing gown around her shoulders. She had seen the clock at midnight then 1:00 a.m. and while Mark snored contentedly beside her, she found the unfamiliar surrounds of the B&B unnerving. The events of the past few days revolved endlessly in her brain and as she guessed at the uncertain resolution to them, the chances of sleep seemed even more remote.

Gently she eased herself from the bed and, slipping on her robe, stepped over to the window. The silent village lay before her. There had been no sound for hours, apart from the occasional isolated chug-chug of a yacht's motor drifting across the chill waters. Now there was nothing to disturb the nocturnal tranquillity.

The pitch-black of the night revealed little of the village. Only the subtle light from the stars betrayed the outline of the church with its ashy coloured spire. Belinda recalled that it had once been used as a watchtower against marauding Vikings. She smiled at the comforting thought of the women and children of the village taking refuge within the church tower during one of the many raids.

She wondered what riches lay beneath the earth before her, lay within the confines of the ancient tomb of the missionary Dicul and his monks, and feared the disturbance of their venerable bones that had been guarding the secret for nigh on a thousand years.

These unpleasant thoughts, along with the frosty air, caused her to shiver violently. With a faint yawn and the suspicion that she could now sleep, Belinda turned to rejoin Mark in the warm bed.

As she did, a movement, caught in the corner of her eye, made her freeze. Turning back, she saw, in the pitch-black of the churchyard, a faint yellow light that floated wraith-like through the impenetrable shadows of the trees.

Nerves tingling with alarm, Belinda watched it drift on its ghostly way towards her. She was about to scream in horror, when she realised that it was the flicker of a lantern, a glow created not by a spirit, but by a man, a man who must have mysterious reasons for approaching the excavations so stealthily.

Mark was indignant at being shaken from a deep comfortable sleep, but was instantly alert when Belinda detailed the activity in the churchyard. They stood at the window looking out into the night. 'Are you sure you weren't dreaming?' demanded Mark curtly, as he observed the apparently deserted churchyard.

'Of course not. And keep your voice down. We don't want our landlady disturbed. I don't want to have to explain to her why we're wandering around a graveyard in the middle of the night.'

'Couldn't it wait 'til morning?' whispered Mark, not attracted to the idea of plodding around the church in the cold night air.

'That's the reason we're here, you nitwit. Not a holiday. I'm willing to bet that's Godwin out there and I want to see what he's up to.'

There was no use protesting. Mark, grumbling under his breath, yielded up his objection. It took only a few minutes for them to dress and, torch in hand, they crept out into the hall. Their quarters were on the opposite side of the house from Mrs O'Brien. The house was in total darkness. They had cautiously inched their way towards the front door when Belinda suddenly shuddered and clasped at Mark.

Something cold and hairy brushed against her leg.

She felt the scream rising in her throat, when a loud meow from Mr Pudding announced his inquisitive presence. With a sigh of relief Belinda gave the cat a firm push with her foot, an action that any cat lover would have identified under oath as a kick, which sent Mr Pudding skidding across the polished floorboards. He gave a cry of bruised dignity, a grievance loud enough to awaken Mrs O'Brien; her drowsy voice was raised in querulous perplexity.

As they hurried to the door, Mark accidentally stood on Mr Pudding's expansive tail. The resulting banshee shriek was loud enough to have woken not only Dicul, but also his accompanying monks. To their dismay, Belinda and Mark saw a sliver of light appear under Mrs O'Brien's bedroom door and heard the ominous creak of bedsprings.

A desperate fumble with the door released them into the night. Carefully they edged their way towards the looming outline of the church.

The path through the graves was difficult at any time. In the shadows of night it became an eerie assault course lined with broken tombstones and hidden crevices. They reached the dig by treading carefully around the protective barrier. Mark clambered down onto the wooden ledge that had been placed around the cavity. He turned and assisted Belinda down the crumbling wall.

Together they peered into the pitch-black opening. They could just make out a rope ladder that disappeared down into the emptiness. Belinda switched on the torch, sending a blade of light that cut through the murky surroundings.

'Put that out,' snapped Mark in an authoritative whisper. He grasped the torch and tore it from Belinda's hand. 'If anyone's here we don't want to advertise our presence.'

Belinda caressed her sore fingers and strained her eyes to see into the hole. She grasped Mark's arm. 'Look,' she whispered, 'down there. There's a faint light. Godwin's down in the crypt.'

Mark leant forward and confirmed there was an imperceptible glow far below. 'Whoever's down there,' he whispered softly in Belinda's ear, 'is below the crypt. It looks as though they have been digging outwards from the vault. Probably into an old gravesite beside the church.'

'Where the monks were buried,' replied Belinda, her teeth chattering from the cold, as well as from apprehension.

As they gazed into the opening, Belinda slowly became aware of a shadow within the shadow. She raised her eyes and in the gloom saw the outline of a man on the level above them. Before she could react, she was blinded by a dazzling brilliance. She fell back against Mark.

As her vision slowly returned to normal she realised the light was coming from a torch that was trained on them both. She heard an all too familiar voice.

'I've had just about enough of your meddling.'

Charles Godwin looked down at them, his eyes filled with bitterness. He jumped down onto their level, the planks moving precariously beneath the three of them.

'Planning another kidnapping?' challenged Mark angrily. He made a move forward but was stopped by Godwin's harsh command.

'I wouldn't make any sudden moves if I were you. Look above you. Brother Saul has you in his sights.'

Belinda felt cold as she turned her eyes upwards. Above her was the faint image of Saul. His face was a mask but his eyes were riveted upon them. He stood above them, strong legs apart, solid, dominating and ruthless. A hunter watching his prey. A movement of his hand revealed the vicious glint of a handgun. He raised it and pointed it at Belinda.

'I imagine you've discovered the secret of the tapestry?' mocked Godwin. 'Clever little thing, aren't you?'

Belinda, angry at herself for being caught, as well as with Godwin for his snide remarks, replied, 'I like to think I am.'

Godwin laughed. 'I'm sorry you and your boyfriend had to show up here. It would have been much better if you'd left things as they were. Now you leave me nothing else to do but to have you disposed of.' He glanced down into the pit. 'But I must say this is a convenient location. You have a ready-made grave.' He stepped back and folded his arms. 'Go ahead, Saul. They are all yours.'

There was a silence broken only by the cry of a distant animal. The three looked up to Saul. He stood above them, like a sinister avenging angel, the revolver pointed rigidly at Belinda and Mark.

Godwin gave a sigh of irritation. 'Get on with it,' he hissed.

Lazily, Saul transferred his arrogant gaze to Godwin. With slow determination he swung the gun in an arc until it was pointing at him. Godwin, bemused, glanced again at Saul. His eyes opened in surprised horror as he saw the gun aimed in his direction. Saul gave a horrible snigger.

Godwin opened his mouth to speak, but the muted blast from the gun silenced him.

His body shuddered and he fell heavily against the low retaining wall. With an unspoken question on his lips he slumped lifeless alongside the damp earth.

Frozen in the nightmare, Belinda clung to Mark. They both dragged their eyes from the dead man to focus on the murderer above them. A malicious smile played on his lips as he swung the gun back again until he had his captives in his sights once more.

Trapped and rigid now with fear, they could do nothing but watch the revolver focus upon them.

Saul's long contorted fingers toyed with the gun's trigger before slowly tightening around it, enfolding it, squeezing it.

Almost as the sound of the discharging bullet filled her ears, Belinda felt Mark hit her between the shoulder blades. He pushed her violently away from him. The savage blow took her breath away and she fell screaming into the black void of the excavation, arms and legs flaying like a deranged puppet.

Once her grasping fingers caught the raw texture of the rope ladder and she clawed at it to halt her plunge into the abyss, but her tentative grip failed as the momentum of her fall compelled her downwards into the grim earth. The piercing edge of a stone coffin tore at her leg. A spray of blood gushed over her.

She seemed to fall forever until suddenly, she landed heavily on a pile of dank soil.

How long she was unconscious she never knew. She gradually became aware of a dull light bleeding through her closed eyelids. Hesitantly she opened her eyes. The bright light of a torch dazzled her. A hand reached out to comfort her.

'Mark!' she cried joyously. He had come to rescue her. She'd make him take her away from all this horror. They would go home to Milford and never think again of that revolting tapestry.

She reached out to take his grasp. As she was drawn upright, she saw his hand was wrinkled like that of an old man. She turned her head and realised his hair had turned white and his features grown sharp and severe.

I'm having a nightmare, she thought, until the cold atmosphere of the engulfing tomb and the pain of her wounded leg brought the realisation that this was reality.

Belinda turned to face her rescuer.

Standing surrounded by looted coffins and a mound of human remains was Sir Gerald.

'You've come just in time for the grand opening. It will probably come as no surprise to you if I tell you that I believe this to be the sarcophagus containing the treasure.'

Desperate thoughts rushed through Belinda's brain.

Had Mark been killed?

How could she escape from Sir Gerald if Saul was at the top of the ladder?

As if in answer to her last question some falling dirt announced the arrival of Saul as he descended the rope ladder. He paused a few rungs from the bottom, hanging above them like a grotesque trapeze artist surveying the scene below.

Sir Gerald drew on heavy leather work-gloves. 'I imagined you'd turn up here sooner or later,' he said to Belinda. 'I realised that after stealing my computer disc, which you did – so don't try and deny it – you would decipher the meaning of the tapestry.' He paused and looked thoughtful. 'I really should never have given you that photograph, it was a stupid mistake. Without it you would never had been clever enough to put two and two together.'

Reaching down he picked up a chisel and a hammer and walked to the huge stone sarcophagus, which stood at a precarious angle against the earthen wall of the excavation.

'I had hoped you would be content to pursue Godwin in the belief that he'd arranged the murders of de Montfort and that idiot Lawson, your one time vicar. If you'd done that, I would have been able to track down the Canterbury treasure in peace.'

Belinda forced herself to speak. 'He didn't kill them?'

Sir Gerald looked surprised. 'Oh, you hadn't realised that was a false trail?' He paused, hammer raised in the air, and surveyed

Belinda with a contemptuous look. 'Perhaps you're not as smart as I thought. No, Godwin was a fool, not a murderer. Descended from the kings of England!' he snorted derisively and shook his head at the apparent stupidity of the man. 'Somewhere along the way he stumbled upon the information that the missing end panel of the Bayeux Tapestry contained instructions to find the treasure. Treasure the monks of Canterbury had hidden. He was my only rival to this knowledge, so it served my purpose that he be suspected of murder.'

Despite her pain – she felt sure she had broken a bone – and regardless of the danger she was in, Belinda felt driven to seek answers to the mystery.

'How did you know about the tapestry being in Kidbrooke House?'

'I'd heard for years that the end panel existed, the rumour had been circulated for centuries and there were countless references to it in mediaeval documents. It was only when I visited de Montfort that I happened upon the square he had framed in his house. It seems it had been tucked away in the attic for years and only recently rediscovered. De Montfort hung it downstairs without imagining its value. When I saw it I realised it must be the missing panel. I offered to purchase it but the fool would not sell, so after trying fair means I had to resort to foul. But I was too late. De Montfort died in vain, because the panel had already disappeared from the house.' He paused and stepped a little closer to Belinda. 'I never did discover how it came into your possession.'

'It was hidden in a drawer of a piece of furniture that was auctioned off from Kidbrooke House.'

Sir Gerald gave an ironic laugh. 'As simple as that? I suppose I should be grateful the Reverend gentleman brought it to me, otherwise I would probably never have known its fate.'

Belinda felt dizzy and massaged her brow. Her head ached from the fall. 'Why are you telling me this?'

'You asked, you stupid girl. Besides, I see no reason for you not to know, because, my dear, you'll be remaining here!' Sir Gerald turned to Saul and gave a faint nod of his head. 'It will teach you not to meddle in things that do not concern you.'

He turned back to begin chipping away at the lid of the sarcophagus. The great stone coffin shuddered insecurely.

Belinda looked up to Saul who was still hanging from the ladder. She saw him produce the gun from his pocket.

The clang of the hammer rang through the crypt as Sir Gerald began to open the stone lid, each reverberation overlapping the other until the tomb vibrated with unearthly sound. Belinda moved away until her back was against the damp wall of the cell. Saul held the gun trained on her as he let go of the rope ladder.

Sir Gerald was distracted by the sudden rush of movement as Saul leapt from the last rungs of the rope ladder and landed beside him. Raising the revolver he fired point blank at Sir Gerald.

The old man, raising his arm in front of his face in a vain attempt to protect himself, took the full force of the blast. He staggered back against the sarcophagus, the weight of his lifeless body knocking the stone receptacle from its rickety base.

It toppled forward and fell.

Saul leapt backwards but not quickly enough, for the heavy stone coffin, glossy with its coating of fresh scarlet blood, caught him and pinned him to the ground. With a scream of pain as his legs were crushed Saul dropped the gun.

Shrieking for Belinda to help, he clawed desperately at the unmoveable weight squashing his limbs, his fingers bloodied as the rough stone tore into his skin.

Belinda stared in horror and felt her gorge rise. The momentum of the fall loosened the stone lid and it fell away. Spilling across the earthen floor rolled a skull and bones, along with mummified dust that was once the living flesh of a holy man.

The screams of the wounded Saul echoed around the vault only to be absorbed into the dank earth, which thirstily drank in his blood.

Frozen in the nightmare setting, Belinda gaped at the violated sarcophagus. Along with the crumbling skeleton there was the glint of tarnished gold, the subdued flash of rubies, the dim gleam of emeralds and the muted glimmer of ancient silver.

The coveted treasures of Canterbury lay finally at Belinda's feet.

Fourteen

'Gold chalices embedded with rubies! Wonderful gold and silver patens and ciboriums. Some exquisite monstrances and beautifully decorated reliquaries, all studded with gems of every description. Plus gold plates of all sizes and a few exquisite crosiers.'

The skeletal remains of Christmas turkey congealed on the table and Belinda spooned the last of the plum pudding into Mark's mouth as she extolled the beauty of the long buried treasure.

Hazel, disregarding the pudding, opened the third bottle of champagne.

Mark and Belinda sat side by side on the sofa. Belinda, her leg heavily bandaged, fed Mark whose right arm was in a sling and his shoulder rigid with bandages. He was dressed in pyjamas and dressing gown. Apart from the discomfort of his wounded shoulder, he seemed to be luxuriating in Belinda's mollycoddling. He rather enjoyed having her in the role of ministering spirit, with himself in the part of wounded saviour. Perhaps it was worth the while being shot – although he could have done without the severe loss of blood and his subsequent stay in hospital. He had willingly succumbed to Belinda's offer to nurse him back to health. These thoughts vanished suddenly as he winced from a spasm of pain that shot through his arm.

'Where are they now?' he grunted, cautiously shifting his body nearer the warmth of the fire.

'The museum authorities got their covetous hands on them. I think they're already planning a huge international exhibition. They can fight it out with the top brass from the Church to see who gets to keep them.'

Belinda rose and placed the empty pudding bowls on the table. She surveyed the ruins of the meal. Knowing that she would have no assistance from Hazel for the rest of the day, she determined that the dishes could wait until tomorrow. She resumed her seat by the fire.

'What I don't understand,' said Hazel, as she handed her a fresh glass of champagne, 'is what was the connection between Sir Gerald and Godwin?'

'There wasn't any, apparently,' replied Belinda. 'From what the police have been able to get from Saul, it seems that he was employed by Sir Gerald purely to put Godwin out of the search. That's why we thought the Godwins were behind the murders.'

Hazel shook her head in disbelief. 'So Saul was the murderer all along. But why?'

'You'd better start from the beginning,' said Mark settling back into the cushions. He'd heard it all before when the police in the hospital ward had interviewed them. Just now, he felt the ennui that follows Christmas dinner rapidly descending upon him.

'Sir Gerald believed that there was a missing panel from the Bayeux Tapestry and he wanted it at all costs, purely from a collector's point of view,' began Belinda. 'He discovered the tapestry square at Kidbrooke House and was determined to get it. Coincidentally, the Godwins discovered it about the same time and Sir Gerald found out.'

'But how?'

'Apparently his friend and old school chum, William de Montfort, let it drop that other people, the Godwins, had offered him money for it, but he let it be known to them, as well as to Sir Gerald, that it was not for sale under any circumstance.

'That's when Sir Gerald employed Saul. He tracked the Godwins down, discovered their obsession with King Harold, and planted Saul within Godwin's community as his spy, with instructions to kill to get the tapestry, but to always make it look as though the killings were instigated by Godwin.'

'And so he went out and slaughtered de Mountjoy?'

'Montfort,' sighed Belinda. 'Apparently that wasn't planned. Saul had gone there under Godwin's instruction to get the tapestry for him.'

'So Saul was working for two masters?'

'Well, each master thought they had Saul's services exclusively. Anyway, de Montfort refused to give it up to Saul. That happened just after we left Kidbrooke House. You remember we saw the monks arguing with the old man.'

'You saw them, dear,' interrupted Hazel. 'I didn't.'

Belinda glared at her. 'Take my word for it, dear. They argued. Not getting his own way, Saul lost his temper and killed him. Bashed him over the head.

'Then, bearing in mind Sir Gerald's instructions, he mutilated him in the same manner as King Henry met his death, gouging out his eye and cutting open his thigh, thinking that eventually it may lead the police back to Godwin.'

'A pretty mixed-up logic, surely?'

'Well I don't think anyone ever suggested that Saul was capable of logic.'

'But why kill the Vicar?'

'Because he knew the truth about my tapestry. Sir Gerald had been excited when it turned up unexpectedly in his house and, overcome with happiness at having it in his possession, blurted out the meaning of the borders. That was one thing he had not expected, a bonus in a way.

'He was more than content just to own a piece of the Bayeux Tapestry but his expertise in iconography proved another bonus when he discovered the borders. If you remember they had been folded out of sight when he'd seen it in its frame at Kidbrooke House. It didn't take him long to piece together the message hidden in the borders. He came to the same conclusion we did, only much sooner of course, that something was buried at Bosham, probably treasure.

'The ironic thing is that if Sir Gerald had not shown off his knowledge about the meaning of the borders, held his tongue instead of spelling everything out for me, I would never have thought about the borders as having any significant meaning.'

'But I still don't see why he had the Vicar killed.'

'When the Vicar returned home Sir Gerald realised his folly in revealing to him that the tapestry was genuine and what message was contained in the border, much the same as he did with me, except in the Vicar's case he told him about the treasure.

'That's why the Vicar was so excited. And because he knew the secret he had to go. Again Saul employed the method that would cast suspicion on Godwin, so the killing took place in the same way that King Harold was slaughtered.'

'How did Sir Gerald ever come in contact with someone like Saul?'

'Apparently he had been active at one stage with criminal rehabilitation and he had known of Saul at that time. He realised Saul would never be reformed so decided that he could use his criminal bent to his own advantage. He paid him well, but what he didn't realise was that Saul had every intention of looking after himself. He planned to take possession once Sir Gerald had discovered the treasure and dispense with him. He was going to make it seem that Godwin was the culprit in that murder as well.

'Saul realised he was on to a good thing at the Godwin's farm and so he sent for all his delinquent mates and they eventually took over the place, which is what upset Mrs Godwin.'

'But why did Saul bash me up? And why search my flat? What was he looking for?' Hazel asked.

Belinda shrugged. 'Who can say? Probably nothing. He might have just got a thrill out of beating you up.'

Hazel pulled a face. 'Charming. So you think he had been following us?'

'I'm certain he followed us when we left Kidbrooke House after the auction. And then he recognised me the day the Godwins first called here at the cottage. He was driving their car. The Godwins were convinced that I knew the whereabouts of the tapestry and so they welcomed me into their community hoping that I would reveal where it was.'

'But who was he following us for? Godwin or Sir Gerald?'

'Initially for himself, I imagine. After all, we, or at least I, could have identified him because I saw him at Kidbrooke House. On the other hand, Sir Gerald would have wanted me watched because he suspected I knew more than I was telling. Godwin probably would have wanted me watched to see if I would reveal where the tapestry square was.'

'But surely the Godwins must have realised Saul was a crook?'

'Yes, they did and Godwin decided to capitalise on the fact. But Saul wasn't going to play second fiddle to any man. Godwin became a nuisance, which's why Saul killed him. He wanted both men out of the way so that he could keep the treasure for himself.'

'Will he recover?'

'The doctors say it's touch and go. He lost a lot of blood and the weight of the sarcophagus did a lot of internal damage apart from crushing his legs. The police did manage to interview him briefly before the doctors called a halt. If he does survive, he'll be crippled for life and of course after his admission of guilt he'll be charged with four murders.'

Hazel gave a shiver of distaste. 'To think he may have had that gun when he attacked me. I hate the bloody things. The sooner they ban them all the better.'

Belinda nodded. 'I'm afraid guns will always be available to criminals when they want them.' They considered this melancholy statement in silence.

'There's one thing you've forgotten,' said Mark, drowsily.

Both women jumped slightly at the sound of his voice.

'I thought you were asleep,' Belinda said in surprise.

'Who could sleep with you rabbiting on,' retorted Mark light-heartedly, as he struggled upright on the cushions.

'Well, what have I forgotten?' inquired Belinda, bridling a little that her summation of the mystery was doubted.

'You haven't explained how Godwin discovered that there was treasure buried at Bosham Church.'

Belinda and Hazel gazed at him. Mark looked smugly from one woman to the other. 'He's right, you know,' muttered Hazel haltingly. She turned her attention to Belinda.

Belinda was at a loss for words. She wracked her brain for inspiration. Her deduction had been based on information gathered from talking to the police and her own knowledge of events supplemented by guesswork. But Mark was right. How did Godwin discover the secret of the tapestry border?

'Well,' she muttered, prepared to improvise, 'I imagine that Godwin suspected the square to be part of the original tapestry when he saw it at Kidbrooke House. That's why he wanted it.'

Mark plumped up a pillow with his good arm. 'But Godwin never got to see it out of the frame. It wasn't out of your hands until you sent it to Sir Gerald and it's certain he wouldn't bandy it about. So how did Godwin know what was on the border?'

'The only way would have been for Saul to have told him,' replied Belinda, not entirely convinced by her own solution.

Mark and Hazel both shook their heads. 'Why would he do that?' asked Hazel.

'Exactly,' agreed Mark. 'If he knew about the treasure, he obviously learnt about it from Sir Gerald, and wanting it for himself, why tell Godwin?'

Belinda gave an irritated shake of her shoulders. Why hadn't she thought of that?

'Well, I expect Inspector Jordan will find out when he interviews Saul again.'

With Christmas behind them, Belinda, Mark and Hazel began to pick up the threads of their life. Mark, when he was fully recovered from his wound, resumed selling property, Hazel started searching out antiques and Belinda began preparing her house for the approaching tourist season.

Belinda telephoned her parents in Australia. As she listened to her mother's voice, she gazed out into the murky twilight and envied them the summer morning just beginning in Melbourne, with its promise of a swim in the warm sea, a picnic in the Dandenong Ranges amongst the myriad green tree ferns, with the delicate chime of the bellbirds filtering through the tall timbers. She really must have a holiday soon. As she hung up the phone she became aware of a deep depression engulfing her and a feeling of dissatisfaction. The medication the doctor had prescribed to calm her after the recent traumas did little to still the unsolved mystery that niggled away in her brain. She knew there would be many sleepless nights in the foreseeable future.

The Godwins' farm lay under a soft blanket of snow as Belinda halted the car beneath the now superfluous Fellowship of St Augustine sign. The unexplained mystery that Mark detected had troubled her for the past week and on New Year's Eve morning, unable to endure the puzzle any longer, she drove to the farm in search of an answer.

A car was parked near the gate and as Belinda stepped out she saw the figure of Mrs Godwin approaching. She carried a large suitcase, which she dropped at Belinda's feet. The two women looked at each other in acrimonious silence.

'I don't think we have anything to talk about.' Mrs Godwin began to load the suitcase into the boot of her car.

'You're leaving?'

'That's stating the obvious,' replied Mrs Godwin in her masculine voice. She slammed the boot closed.

'I'm sorry about your husband,' said Belinda.

'I'm not,' snapped Mrs Godwin, 'I think you know what I thought of Charles. So if you're here to offer sympathy, forget it.'

'Actually, I'm here for another reason,' said Belinda hurriedly, as Mrs Godwin brushed past her and seated herself in the car.

'As I said,' replied Mrs Godwin, slamming the door, 'I don't think we have anything to say to each other.'

'Mrs Godwin. I know you are upset, but you're not the only one hurt by all this. The Vicar, who was my friend, was murdered. And, frankly, I've been through hell myself,' she concluded angrily.

Mrs Godwin wound the window down and looked up at Belinda. 'You lost a friend. I lost a husband. And what's more, I lost a father.'

Belinda stared at her.

'You'll be surprised to hear that Sir Gerald Taylor was my father,' continued Mrs Godwin, her voice breaking with restrained emotion. 'Not a very good father, I admit. We couldn't be in each other's company for more than five minutes, then we'd be at each other's throat. It had always been like that even when my mother was alive.

'We were opposites in every way. He criticised everything I did. My choice of clothes, boyfriends, career. In turn, I hated his smug authority and his overbearing priggishness. Frankly I wonder why he ever had a child. He disapproved of my marriage to Charles and would have nothing to do with us. But – he was all the family I had. And now I have nothing. No one.'

Belinda was speechless.

'So now you know, and if you don't mind, I'd like you get out of the way and let me leave. I've told the police all I know and there is nothing for me here any more.'

'Where will you go?' asked Belinda, finding her voice with difficulty.

The woman looked at her. 'I'm staying in Bath until all this is over, I mean the trial, if there is to be one. After that? Who knows? Europe? America? I don't know. All I do know is that I never want to see this place ever again.' She looked Belinda full in the face. 'Or you, for that matter.'

She turned and switched on the ignition. The motor sprang into life. Belinda reached out and took hold of the car door.

'Please. Just one thing before you go. Can you tell me how your husband found out about the treasure hidden at Bosham? I know he was obsessed with the Bayeux Tapestry and with King Harold, but there was nothing there that could have led him to the treasure.'

Mrs Godwin turned off the ignition and in the sudden hush turned to Belinda. 'Is that all you've got to worry about?'

Belinda felt a wave of irritation pass over her. 'Mrs Godwin,' she said firmly, 'the only indication that there was treasure buried at the church was given in the scrap of tapestry that came from Kidbrooke House. I know your husband wanted it and now it's missing. Did he have it and do you have it now?'

Mrs Godwin shook her head slowly. 'The answer is no to both questions. Yes he wanted it, but he knew nothing about the treasure. It was only after he learned about the cursed thing that he changed. Changed into a madman. Obsessed with finding it.'

'Then he did have the tapestry.'

'No. He saw a photograph of it.'

Belinda stared in amazement. 'But how would he have got hold of the photograph? I had it. Sir Gerald … your father gave it to me.'

Mrs Godwin smiled shrewdly. 'He gave you one photograph. He had several. I called on him one day, to try and patch up our relationship. We may have hated each other but – he was my father – and the world is full of too much hate. I hadn't seen him for some years and I thought that time and old age might have mellowed him. But I was wrong. He was as hateful as ever.

'He wanted nothing to do with me. He had come to loathe Charles and, I now realise, wanted him dead. We had a vicious fight. He failed to understand that what ever Charles may have been, I loved him, and my father envied that love because he could never generate love for himself.

'I saw the photographs on his desk and in a moment of spite I took them, mainly to antagonise my father, but also because I thought it would interest Charles. They looked like a piece of the damned Bayeux Tapestry he was obsessed with. Little did I know that my father was as obsessed.' She wiped tears from her eyes. 'It drove my husband to distraction. With his knowledge it was easy for him to decipher the borders and to realise what they meant. From that time on he was a madman. So you see, my dear, it was I who sowed the seeds of that madness.'

She switched on the ignition once more and, with a last antagonistic look at Belinda, drove away.

Belinda watched her go until the car was out of sight and soft flakes of snow began to fall.

'The strange thing is that I saw her at Winchester the day I called on Sir Gerald.'

Belinda was retelling her encounter with Mrs Godwin to Mark and Hazel. It was New Year's Eve and, under the circumstances, they were planning a quiet welcome to the New Year. 'You saw her?' queried Mark.

Belinda nodded. 'The same day he gave me the photograph. I saw her leave the railway station. She must have visited her father just after I'd left and she would have seen the other photographs on his desk.'

Hazel rose and drew the curtains. The hazy evening light was failing and the clouds hung heavy with snow. She switched on the lamps.

The colour photograph taken by Sir Gerald of the tapestry square lay on the coffee table and she picked it up and looked at it under the glow of the reading lamp. 'Did you find out what happened to your tapestry?'

Belinda shrugged and shook her head. 'No one knows. It's vanished again. The police have searched Sir Gerald's house, his security box at the bank, everywhere.'

'Did they look at Godwin's farm?' asked Hazel, warming herself by the fire.

Belinda sank down onto the sofa and hugged a cushion to her breast. 'They looked. But it wasn't there. Mrs Godwin claims it never was. And now she's gone too.' She gave a bemused sigh. 'It's nowhere to be found. Perhaps in another nine hundred years or so it will turn up again and there'll be even more murders.

Hazel placed the photograph on sofa. 'You should frame this, you know. At least you'll have a memento even though you don't have the original.'

Belinda reached down and, taking the photograph, threw it forcefully into the fire.

'I wish I'd never seen it in the first place.'

The flames eagerly licked the snapshot and, ignorant of its significance, rapidly consumed it until all that remained was ephemeral grey ash, ash that had flared for one brief bright moment before succumbing to inevitable decay.

The End

Also Available from BeWrite Books

Capable of Murder by Brian Kavanagh

The old lady's decaying body lay at the foot of the stairs.

The police believe it was simply an accidental fall that killed great-aunt Jane.

But was it?

Young Australian, Belinda Lawrence is convinced it was murder and when she inherits her great-aunt's ancient cottage and garden on the outskirts of Bath, England, she finds herself deep in a taut mystery surrounding her legacy.

A secret room. Unknown intruders. A hidden ancient document. They all contribute to the mounting dread.

A second vicious murder by a ruthless killer intensifies the tension and Belinda, now under threat herself, is befriended by two charming men: her neighbour Jacob and real-estate agent Mark Sallinger. But can she trust them? And what interest has befuddled antique dealer Hazel Whitby in the cottage?

Could one of them be the killer?

An excellent example of a time-honoured English village murder mystery with a lively young heroine pitting her intellect against an evil killer, both bent on solving the riddle of an ancient garden.

An inventive puzzle glazed with wit and the first of the Belinda Lawrence series.

Paperback ISBN 1-905202-10-5

With interesting characters, Brian Kavanagh's well-crafted, seductive tale, Capable of Murder lulls the reader into a false sense of security then attacks when least expected. There are many twists and turns as the story winds its way toward its startling conclusion.
This is a must-read book. It is definitely recommended.
Nancy Madison, author of 'Clues to Love'

Mr Kavanagh managed to do what one of my favorite authors, M C Beaton, does so well, incorporate humor within the confines of a credible mystery.
Mary Lynn, author of 'Dear Cari'

BeWrite Books

Also Available from BeWrite Books

The Adventures of Alianore Audley by Brian Wainwright

Alianore Audley is a good, submissive, demure woman of the fifteenth century … and if you believe that, you'll believe anything. But she is a spy in Edward IV's intelligence service, and the author of a chronicle that casts – well, a new light, let's say, on the times of the Yorkist kings. History will never be the same after Alianore. Nor will most other novels.

A wonderful romp set in 15th-century England. Told with zest, a deep love and knowledge of the period … a wicked sense of humour and plenty of tongue in cheek … Wainwright deserves far greater recognition …
Elizabeth Chadwick's Top 10 Historical Novels, The Guardian

Paperback ISBN 1-904492-78-9

Evil Angel by RD Larson

Beautiful Terri has a heavenly face … and the heart of an evil angel.

When her husband walks out on her insane jealousies and fantasies, the Evil Angel becomes real to Terri – materialising to guide her on a path of manic violence and death.

Meanwhile a true love story is becoming a reality – a reality the Evil Angel in her bloodlust and obsession with revenge will stop at nothing to destroy.

This no-holds-barred page-turner of twisted love and lethal vengeance races through to a stomach-punch of a climax that will leave the reader breathless.

Paperback ISBN 1-904224-82-2

BeWrite Books